Tangled Trail

A Mary O'Reilly World Paranormal Mystery

By
Donnie Light

Copyright 2016 by Donnie Light

All rights reserved. No portion of this book may be reproduced in any form without permission from the publisher, except as permitted by U.S. copyright law.

This is a work of fiction. Names, characters, businesses, places, events, locales, and incidents are either the products of the author's imagination or used in a fictitious manner. Any resemblance to actual persons, living or dead, or actual events is purely coincidental.

2108-0728

Foreword

Hi! This is Terri Reid, author of the Mary O'Reilly Paranormal Mystery series. The author of this book has my permission to use the characters and world of the Mary O'Reilly Series. I hope you enjoy this adventure into alternate Mary O'Reilly realities.

—Terri Reid

Dedication

For Barbara and Adam, who are always there for me with encouraging words and accurate assessments. Stories do not exist without readers, and I thank you for your roles in creating this story.

In loving memory of Dustin; I miss you, man…

Acknowledgements

I am excited to be a part of the *Mary O'Reilly Paranormal Mystery* World, and thank friend and amazing author, **Terri Reid**, for creating the vibrant body of work that inspired this World.

Thanks to **Ophelia Julien**, author of the *Bridgeton Park Cemetery Books*. I've spent many hours talking ghosts and the paranormal with Ophelia and Terri Reid, and it was they who took me on my first Ghost Tour, in Galena, Illinois.

Niki Danforth, the author of the *Ronnie Lake Mystery* books, who in the middle of editing her own next novel, took time to read on comment on this book. Thanks, Niki.

Prologue

If you take the county road west of the village of Willow River, Illinois, and watch closely, you will find a narrow gravel lane snaking its way between tall oak and cedar trees. The path eventually comes to a dusty stop at a couple of old, Victorian-style houses. The name of the road is Tangled Trail, and this name perfectly matches its character.

The two houses sit side-by-side, like a pair of elderly patients sharing a hospital room. The older house, on the left, is more rundown than the other. It's the one where I spent most of my life.

The homes were built over eighty-five years ago by a man who made a lot of money early in his career. Back in 1930, that man bought sixty acres, half of which was dense woods. The contractor wanted to clear a wide lane to the building site, but the owner insisted on cutting down as few trees as possible, then called the result, a tangled trail. The name never changed.

We moved there fifteen years ago, when I was only three, so I'm not sure if my first memories of the house are real, or something fabricated from stories I heard. But I remember gazing at the large, dark house with a sense of awe.

A friendly lady with a gold jacket talked to my parents while I stood in the back seat of the car, staring at the highest windows. Birds danced in the air around the eaves as I wondered how far I could see if I were looking out those dark, dirty windows.

My dad carried me as we toured the house. I recall the echo of the sales lady's heels clicking on the hardwood floors as she jabbered on; my parents asking questions and nodding politely in response to her answers.

When we moved in, my parents didn't have enough furniture to fill the large rooms. Many sat empty except for the cobwebs and dust. But my mom and dad had plans. They had ambition and energy—and the big dreams of young love.

I have early memories of our only neighbor, Miss Anna DuVall, who always seemed to like me, and who often comforted me. She lived in the house next door, a few years newer than our house, but in the same basic style of construction and size. Her father was the wealthy young man who built the houses so long ago.

Memories of going next door for oatmeal-raisin cookies and Kool-Aid while my parents went to town are so clear in my mind. Miss Anna, (I always called her *Miss Anna*, but how that started I do not recall) would often put worn cigar boxes full of old photos on the table and tell me stories about what was happening when a particular photo was taken. Fourth of July seemed a popular time for the DuVall family to snap pictures, along with Christmas and Easter.

Many of the photos had been trimmed with scissors, as if to cut a subject out of the picture, which I always found odd. Some of those images are burned into my mind so deeply that I can recall tiny details; like the small hand or part of a white shoe that was missed by the scissor-wielding editor.

Miss Anna would not talk about why the photos were snipped, or who was missing from the original image. She often became strangely quiet when I questioned her about it. Her eyes would glaze over and stare at nothing, so I eventually stopped asking.

Miss Anna and I grew closer over the years. She always welcomed me when I had trouble at home, her kitchen becoming a refuge of sorts. We almost always looked at those pictures when we were together. It was like an illustrated storytime.

As I got older, the contrast between how the houses appeared in the old photos and what they had become grew more apparent. In the old pictures, I saw what once were grand, colorful country homes where children ran barefoot on the lawn and a Model A Ford sat in the gravel driveway. Where a grove of bountiful fruit trees once grew—apple, pear and black walnut —was now a patch of twisted snags and gnarled stumps. Miss Anna's pictures (although black and white) showed brightly painted houses that were now just hulking gray boxes with leaking roofs and broken TV antennas leaning awkwardly toward the sky. The grass, full and thick in the old photos was now sparse and sickly, like a threadbare rug.

As I compared what I saw in real life to what I saw in the photos, I always wondered what had happened on Tangled Trail. What caused the life and brightness of days gone by to devolve into this current state of decay?

I could not have known then what I have learned since. And to be honest, I believe it all had to happen the way it did. It was like a destined plan that would change the lives of every person who lived on Tangled Trail.

My dad once said, "Hadlee, don't think of fear as your enemy. It's more like a compass, pointing out things you need to overcome."

Perhaps somebody famous said that. I don't think Dad made it up, because he was not all that creative with words.

Dad understood me better than anyone else. He knew of my paralyzing fear and always encouraged me to move past it the best way possible. He had hopes that I'd be normal someday; able to move about and fully engage in life. I think he would be proud of my progress.

Although I miss my dad and my mom, I'll never wish that things would go back to the way they were. The first eighteen years of my life were spent in darkness and isolation, and I understand now that I made it that way myself. My entire childhood was spent being afraid of a lot of things that I have since learned were never the threat I perceived them to be.

We all endure struggles in life, and we all have to find our own way past them. With enough determination, we will muster through. Truly, that's the essence of life; *overcoming*. I believe it's the conflicts in life that create our character and open our souls to become bigger than we suppose possible.

I also believe in ghosts…

Chapter 1

For most girls my age, High School Graduation is a big event. For me, it was simply tearing open an envelope from the State that said I had satisfactorily completed my home-schooling curriculum. There was an Internet address where I could login and create my own diploma for only $29.95 and officially be recognized as part of the Class of 2015.

My parents were always broke, so I opted to create my own diploma and print it out at home. It would not be official; but I wanted to touch and feel that worthless piece of paper just the same. I had worked really hard for it. The transcript the State sent was just ugly, not suitable to hang on a wall.

With the graphics program on my computer and a free Old-English font downloaded from the Internet, I got started. There were pictures of diplomas online that I modeled mine after. In just a short time, the diploma was in my hands. Fancy parchment paper would have been nice, but all I had was the cheap, white printer paper my mom used for her work.

The diploma would not be complete without a frame, so I began looking around. There was a fourth-grade picture of me hanging in the hallway with a cheap, metal frame from the Dollar Store in town.

That picture brought back a flood of memories, none of which were pleasant. It was the last school photo that had been taken of me. I wore an awkward grin in the photo, and my auburn hair had been bobbed short at the time. After fourth grade, I never went to a regular school again.

"Nobody will even notice this picture is gone," I said to Lizzy. She meowed, then continued licking her left paw.

After sliding the cardboard from the back of the frame, I discovered my diploma was too big to fit. I dug around in the junk drawer for a pair of scissors, then got to work carefully trimming it down. Lizzy began pawing at the scraps of paper that trailed behind me as I worked.

"This is hard enough without your help," I told her, pushing her aside. She leapt from the desk to the chair, complained with agitated cat-chatter, then curled up for another nap.

I held the completed diploma out at arm's length. It looked good to me, so I carried it toward the front of the house to show my dad.

Our house was not laid out in any traditional fashion. My dad had a room near the front of the house that he called his den. He had a computer and TV in there, a desk that he made out of an old door and milk crates, and a couch. His den was always a total mess. Broken electronics, old video tapes and piles of books and magazines littered the room.

I heard the sounds of phasers firing in rapid succession as I approached Dad's den. He saw me enter his room and held up his index finger, barely glancing from the TV. The *U.S.S Enterprise* was in a battle with a Klingon Bird of Prey, and it looked like the *Enterprise* was getting its butt kicked.

I moved some dirty clothes that were scattered on the couch to make room to sit down. I watched my dad as he watched an episode of *Star Trek–The Next Generation*. He was totally wrapped up in the show, having seen this episode enough times that he was lip-syncing the commands Captain Picard was shouting, while gripping the arms of his chair as if he were sitting in the Captain's seat.

Tangled Trail

Just when Picard gave the order to fire the photon torpedoes, the channel went to commercials.

"This is a good one," Dad said.

He was right; it was a good one. I had watched it with him who knows how many times. I grew up watching *Star Trek, TNG* with my dad, and we both proudly considered ourselves Trekkies.

I help up my diploma.

Dad squinted to read what it said, then grinned when he realized what it was.

"You did it!" he said, holding up his hand for a high-five. "Didn't I always say you would do it?"

And yes, he had always said that.

He held up the frame. "Did you print this out?" he asked.

I nodded. "I designed it myself."

"It's really good," he said.

I nodded again and reached for the diploma. He handed it over with a smile.

Star Trek came back on and he turned his attention to the TV.

"Way to go, kiddo," he said as I left the room.

I expected more of a reaction. Dad seemed less than enthusiastic about the biggest thing I had ever accomplished. As I walked back to my room, I promised myself I would not... but I did.

I began to cry.

When that feeling comes over me, I can't help myself. I flopped onto my bed and sobbed. Tears washed over my face and I did everything I could to stop. Crying was so irrational, but this feeling was like a monster with huge teeth that just overwhelmed me. I knew my dad would never intentionally try to hurt me. He simply didn't respond like I expected him to. Normal people dealt with things like this all the time. But normal people didn't react like I did.

That was just one of my anxiety issues. It was the reason I seldom left home, and never returned to regular school.

I felt weight on my legs as Lizzy crawled over me. She stopped right beside my head. She had been through this so many times that it was just a part of our routine. She had a calming effect on me, so I reached up and stroked her head. She purred loudly.

A few minutes had passed when I saw a shadow fall across the wall. I turned to the door to find my dad standing there, leaning against the frame.

"I'm really sorry, Sweetie," he said. "You okay?"

I gave a weak smile. "Yeah, same as always." I reached for a tissue. "It's not your fault, I know you didn't mean to. It's just my crazy, malfunctioning brain again."

"Have you given any more thought to group therapy?"

"No way," I said. "I'll figure out something else." The thought of group therapy was something that took my anxiety to Alert Level Red.

Dad looked at his watch. "I have an auction ending in like two minutes," he said. "I've got to get back to work. "You sure you're okay?"

I waved him on.

We had all dealt with my anxiety issues since my teacher and principal called my parents to school after my first real anxiety attack. I had always been shy, but I could function. I did my homework. I had friends and played hopscotch at recess with some other girls. But on that one day, everything changed.

I froze in class after being called on by my teacher. The kids laughed, thinking I was ignoring the teacher's question. I melted into my seat, broke out in a sweat and felt flush. Mrs. Camp called the nurse, then the principal. It became a big scene.

I was taken to a number of doctors, counselors and the like, including psychiatrists. None of them agreed completely on what was going on with me, so they labeled me with things like General Anxiety Disorder, Social Anxiety Disorder and Panic Disorder.

The problem was, I didn't fit any of those completely, and exhibited symptoms of them all.

Since those days, my parents and I dealt with it as best we could. Mom thought it was all in my head, and that if I simply decided to, I could move past it. I wish it were that simple.

Dad was different. I think he understood better than anyone what I was going through. He never seemed to doubt the fear I felt at times.

My father really was a kind and decent man. He was quite smart, but I'll admit, he was always somewhat lazy. He had never held onto a job for very long, so he tried to make money by selling things on eBay. He would go to garage sales, factory closeouts, liquidations sales and the like, finding things he could buy cheap and sell online for a profit. He never made much money at it.

Mom was a real estate agent, and she was often out showing houses in the evening, when potential buyers were off work. Business had been slow for months. Mom blamed it on the economy, and she blamed the poor economy on the President.

It was mid-March, and darkness came early. I was in my winter bedroom, which was on the first floor of the house. The house was big and drafty, so in the winter months Dad would close off the second floor to save money on heat.

In the summer I slept on the second floor where I could look out the high windows and catch a cool breeze after sunset. Dad let me paint my summer room one year, the first really big project that I did entirely by myself. Dad found white paint at a liquidation sale and said that white paint would go with any room décor...like I had any décor to be concerned about. I had a single bed, one old chest of drawers, a little table, and a desk where I kept my computer. The floors were bare hardwood with a *Hello Kitty* rug that Dad bought me years before. It had grown on me, so it was still there.

My winter room was smaller and had a single, narrow window that faced the east. Not only was that window constantly frosted over during the winter, but it also lit the room harshly as the sun came up. There was no blind to mute that early brightness, so I hung a towel over the bottom half of the window, which only helped a little.

Dad said that as best as he could tell, my winter room used to be a laundry room. There was a pair of doors that closed off something like a closet. Inside that closet were some old, rusty pipes that came up through the floor from the basement. I thought of them as the source of the spiders and other bugs that crept up the walls and across the ceiling, seeking the warmer climes of the human realm.

Dad was good with computers and other electronics, which is how I learned so much about them. He was always willing to show me how to do things, and when I was fourteen, he helped me build a computer out of the spare parts he had collected. We took a motherboard out of one old computer, a hard drive out of another, and we found a video card for really cheap on eBay. He let me take the parts out and explained what each part did as I put them in my own computer. He then taught me how to maintain a computer properly so that it would always run fast.

I seemed to understand computers much better than I understood people.

That computer was my connection to the outside world. I spent hours reading articles on the Internet, and sometimes spying on people through social media. I guess it wasn't really spying, since they voluntarily put the information out there, but it felt like spying since I never commented or posted anything.

I loved seeing what normal people did with their time. I studied the photos they shared, the stories they told about their lives, and the people they hung out with. I longed to be normal like them, and would imagine a photo of me someday, with my arms around a friend, or just being seen amongst other people. To me, that was a far-away fantasy that I could not really see happening, but it was fun to dream.

After browsing some Internet sites, I sat down at my computer that night to do some writing in my journal. My journal was (and still is) very important to me. It's a place where I can explore my problems and fears without exposing them to anyone else. My journal is simply a file on my computer that contains my innermost truths. I back it up onto a flash drive that I keep hidden in an encrypted file that nobody else can open.

Like every other night, after I finished writing my thoughts in my journal, I did a little preventive maintenance on my old computer.

I closed out my word-processor and the screen went totally white, which was unusual. I thought the computer had perhaps hung up (which was not all that unusual) and that I might need to reboot.

As I reached for the power button, I noticed something very unusual. On that stark white screen, glowing in my darkened room, a dark handprint appeared. It was very subtle; just a shade darker than the white, but it was there. At first, I thought maybe it was my imagination, but as I stared, the delicate handprint grew more pronounced.

I wondered if a computer virus had somehow gotten past my defenses, but I had never heard of a virus that put a hand print on the screen. I looked over my shoulder to see if my dad might be standing in my doorway, having played a good trick on me. The doorway was empty, a cobweb gently billowing in one corner.

I turned back to the computer and saw the handprint move. It lifted away from the screen, as if someone was on the other side of the glass, pulling their hand away.

I then noticed movement in the upper-left corner of the screen. A vertical line, about the width of a finger, slowly descended.

Again, it was a very subtle change in color, a very light gray against the white. The descending line turned to the right.

Frozen in my chair, my mind struggled to make sense of what I was seeing. It had to be some kind of trick or some malfunction in my monitor. But this had never happened before, and my heart was suddenly racing.

I slid my chair back and refocused on the screen.

I now saw a single word scrawled in awkward letters:

LIES.

I reached for the power button and held it in with my eyes closed, counting the seconds. Finally, the sound of the fan and the hard drive stopped and the computer went silent. I looked at the dark screen and saw the ghostly word still faintly glowing in the center and convinced myself that it really wasn't there.

I grabbed Lizzy off the bed, then went and sat with my dad watching *Dr. Who* reruns until my mom came in the back door.

Chapter 2

I know I have not led a normal life to this point. Because of my anxiety disorder, I don't know a lot of people. But I do watch TV and I read books. I have some idea of what *normal* is.

My mom was pretty normal. She was certainly energetic, always looking for something to do. She rarely took any down-time to herself... or so I thought. I believed that, right up to the bitter end when it was revealed to be untrue.

Mom was a doer. She held a job and made enough money to keep our house on Tangled Trail afloat. She cooked dinners ahead of time so there was always something in the fridge for me and Dad. We seldom ate dinners together, as Mom kept odd hours at work.

Mom and Dad were very different people. I often wonder how they ever got together, but as they say, opposites attract.

Mom had bought into Dad's idea of buying the big old house and turning it into a Bed and Breakfast, which would have been the perfect work-at-home job for my dad. I could totally see him greeting guests and keeping things in order if that were his job. He just wasn't much for punching a time clock.

If their plan had worked, it would have been total hell for me. I would have had to hide in my own house, making sure to avoid any strangers wandering through the halls.

Maybe it was because of my condition that Mom and Dad never pursued opening the Bed and Breakfast.

If that was the case, then I love them for their sacrifice.

I know Mom was more affected by my condition than Dad ever was. She could never take me shopping, for instance. No girl's night out with her daughter. No school plays or dance recitals. And certainly, no softball games or prom dresses to buy. I know it was not easy for her. She always seemed to think there was some magical button that could be pushed that would make me normal. It was always Mom who pushed me to go to therapy and seek the advice of various doctors and counselors, but none of that ever worked.

***

Mom came in from work while I was hiding out in Dad's den, still freaked out about the handprint and message on my computer. I heard the back door open and the wave of cold air put goosebumps on my arms.

"Have you ever heard of a virus that does funny things to your screen?" I asked my dad.

He glanced up and to his left, accessing the part of his brain that would recall such things. "I'm sure there must be," he said. "Did you have something happen?"

"Yeah, just a weird image on a blank screen," I said.

"Porn?"

"God no, Dad!" I said, horrified that he would bring that up. I looked away, wondering where Mom was. "It was just a faint handprint." I left out the message that followed.

Dad wondered about it for a moment. "Is your virus protection up to date?"

"Yes, of course."

"Then do a manual scan and see if it turns up anything. Check the website for updates, too."

I nodded but didn't want to even turn my computer on until daylight. It had seriously given me the creeps.

Mom walked into the den with an attitude. "Tomorrow is garbage day, and I didn't see the container out by the road."

"I forgot," Dad said. "I'll go do it now."

He got up from his chair, but hesitated for a moment, leaning heavily on the chair back. He had always been a few pounds overweight, had high blood pressure, and was a borderline diabetic.

"I'll get it," I said. I could tell he was not feeling well.

"Thanks, Sweetie," he said. "I'm just feeling kind of blah at the moment."

Just as I got up, Mom started in on Dad. "You sit here all day messing around and watching TV, and you can't remember the one thing you have to do…"

I left, knowing her routine well enough to know how she would explain that she works hard, earns all the money, so on and so forth. It was her way of complaining and belittling him a bit. It never changed anything, but I understood her frustration.

The garage at the old house was detached, so I had to walk through the cold and dark and push open the door that always stuck. I fought my way in then hoisted the overhead door from the inside, because the handle had broken off on the outside. Dad said he would fix it when the weather warmed up.

I tilted the garbage container onto its wheels and began dragging it toward the road. I was wishing that I had put up my hood when the cold air found its way down my back. I parked the container and turned back to the house, pulling my hood up as I walked when I noticed the light from my room spill out onto the yard. It abruptly went back off, then back on.

I looked at the window, which was frosted over, but there were no shadows moving about.

I quickened my pace to the garage, put down the door and hurried to the house.

I entered through the kitchen, and found Mom and Dad there having coffee. Dad always took his pills while they both had coffee, because Mom knew he wouldn't remember otherwise. She put all of his pills into a container that had his AM and PM doses for each day.

"Was one of you just in my room?" I asked.

"We've been sitting here since you went out," Mom said.

Dad tilted his head back to swallow another pill.

"The light in my room was flashing on and off," I said. "I saw it from the driveway."

Dad took a sip of coffee. "The bulb is probably loose," he said. "I'll go check it in a minute."

I sat down because I was not going to my room alone. A creepy feeling had settled into me, like when you wake up from a nightmare wondering if the monster was still in the closet.

Dad finished his coffee and stood up. "Are you waiting for me?"

I nodded and fell in line behind him as he headed down the hall. The door to my room opened with a squeal which sounded even more hideous than usual. He reached for the switch, clicked it on, and the room filled with light. He stepped fully into the room while I waited in the doorway. Dad looked up at the light fixture.

"Seems okay now," he said. "Turn it on and off a couple of times."

I did, and it worked fine. I stared at the frosted globe that covered the bulbs and took notice of a couple of dead bugs, silhouetted inside.

"It should be fine," Dad said. "I'll change the bulb if it acts up again."

I flicked the switch a couple of times, willing with all my being that it would fail.

It worked fine.

I followed Dad back down the hall, hoping he was going to stay up for a while. Mom went to bed, but Dad stayed in his den with the TV on low while he did some work online. He didn't seem to mind when I fell asleep on his couch.

Chapter 3

I woke up on Dad's couch after a night of really weird dreams. He had covered me with an afghan before he went to bed, and I pulled it tightly around me. I know I must have let the weirdness of the night before get to me—filling my head with strange thoughts.

Lizzy had curled herself around my feet and complained when I adjusted myself. I reached for her and pulled her up close, finding comfort in her soft purring.

But it was a new day, so I decided to just chalk up the handprint and flashing light to coincidence and go on as if nothing had happened.

I heard papers shuffling at the kitchen table. Mom was going through her paperwork for the day. Our house had become filled with endless days that were always the same. The routine became rather boring, and now I had no schoolwork to occupy my time. That reminded me that I had not shown Mom my new diploma, so I grabbed it and met her in the kitchen.

I handed it to her.

"A diploma?"

"Yep."

"Did the State send this to you?"

"No," I said as I put bread in the toaster. "I made it myself. The State wanted to charge $29.95 to send me a copy."

Mom put the diploma to the side, amongst the other papers on the table.

"What are you going to do now?" she asked.

I shrugged, knowing what was coming next.

"You have to do *something*," she said. "You can't just spend your entire life in this house…"

"I know, Mom. I just graduated yesterday. I'll come up with a plan."

"You have been saying that for months, and yet you don't know what you are going to do?"

An uncomfortable silence fell between us as I buttered my toast. As I have said, Mom is a doer, and not much of a nurturer. She thought anyone with an anxiety disorder should just suck it up and walk out the door, ready to take on the world; like learning to swim by being tossed in the deep end of the pool. She never realized the dread I felt when confronted by strangers. How I struggled to breathe with my heart hammering, basically unable to utter a single coherent word. How my legs got too weak to hold me up and it was all I could do just to remain upright.

It was all in my head, she often said.

Of course, she was right. I never argued that point.

"I could maybe get you on at the office doing computer work," she offered. "You are good with computers and you…"

"I'm not ready for that," I said. I was nervous just thinking about going out every day, being in traffic with strange people all around, sitting in an office with people coming and going all day long. I would be frozen in place, unable to focus on anything but the blur of activity around me and the fear I felt.

"You have until the end of the month to come up with a plan," Mom said.

Mom also liked deadlines.

I ate my toast while she finished organizing her papers.

Mom left a few minutes later, leaving me alone in the kitchen. Dad often slept late because he stayed up working his eBay site. He was more nocturnal than Mom and I, saying he liked the dark and the quiet in the middle of the night.

Tangled Trail

The sun was shining through the windows, the trees were still, and it was supposed to be warmer today. Spring was making a nervous showing in the middle of March, as if testing the waters before diving in.

***

I knew Miss Anna would be up, so I decided to go visit her for a while.

Miss Anna was the one person outside of Mom and Dad who I was comfortable with. I had known her since I was small, and more importantly, I had known her since before my disorder manifested. Talking to her was so different than talking to my parents. Miss Anna and her house was like my other world—a place I could go and be comfortable that was outside of my own house.

I started to knock on her kitchen door, only to find her standing there waiting for me.

"I saw you coming," she said in her weak voice. "What are you thinking going out with just a sweater on? You must be freezing."

I took my shoes off at her back door—a rule at her house. "It's not that cold out," I said, "and it was just across the yard."

"Sit, sit," she demanded as she pulled out a kitchen chair.

I reached into the front of my sweater and pulled out my diploma. I held it out to her.

She glanced at it, then put on her reading glasses. "Oh, my," she said. "Well, congratulations are in order. You have graduated!"

There was genuine joy in her voice. You cannot fake joy like that, and it made me happy to know she cared.

She placed the diploma on the table and gave me a hug.

"I'm so proud of you," she said. Miss Anna always smelled of perfume, even when she was still in her robe.

"I baked some snickerdoodle cookies yesterday," she said. She went to her cupboard and retrieved a Tupperware container. "Is it too early for Kool Aid? Would you prefer milk?"

"Kool Aid is fine," I said. It was a ritual we had done so many times that drinking milk would seem sacrilegious.

The funny thing about the conversations between Miss Anna and I was that we had so little to talk about other than ourselves. My dad always said that Miss Anna had come from old money, and he often wondered how much she had left. She had never had to work, had no living relatives, and spent much of her adult life volunteering at the local hospital. She had not volunteered since I could remember, but she told me the stories.

Her father had been a wealthy banker who had the foresight to avoid risk during the great depression. Miss Anna told me many times how her father had seen the depression coming, and had taken steps to protect his assets. He retained and even increased his wealth during that time. Her father had died decades ago. She had sold his original house—my house now—to another family. The house she lived in was also built by her father. It was to have been a wedding present to her when she got engaged as a young woman. The wedding had never happened, but Miss Anna moved into the new house alone, and lived there ever since.

Miss Anna didn't talk much about that. It was easy to see that it was painful for her, and she clammed up when the conversation drifted that way. She told me he was a handsome man, charming and dashing, but a bit wild at times.

Miss Anna had a twin sister, named Emma, who left when she was young. Miss Anna never heard from her again. When Miss Anna told stories of the old days, her eyes would often mist up. It was obvious that she missed her family, and especially her twin sister.

Miss Anna stood and reached for my hand. "Come," she said. "I have something for you."

In all the years that I had known Miss Anna, we had never gone upstairs in her house. She led me to the stairway. Her house was less cluttered than mine, and while the flooring and paint were old, they still held some of their original charm. We climbed the staircase and she led me to a room at the end of the hall.

The room had twin beds on either side, the paint a faded pink. A large braided rug covered the space between the beds. There was a pair of tall windows that looked north. A table sat below the windows, and on that table stood a glorious little doll house.

"Emma and I shared a room when we were little," Miss Anna said. "We could have had our own rooms, of course," she continued, "but when we were young we didn't want to be separated." She produced a pitiful little laugh, and her eyes got that misty look. "Not even for a night."

I stared at the little doll house. It wasn't very big and looked to have been hand-made. There were two little rooms upstairs and three down. The kitchen had a little wooden table and white stove. The living room held a couch and chair, and the dining room contained a table and china cabinet. The floors had rugs painted on the them.

In the upstairs bedrooms were tiny beds and two porcelain dolls, both girls. One was dressed in green and the other in yellow.

"It was our favorite toy," Miss Anna said. "The green doll is Emma," she said. "The yellow one is me." She showed me how the back of the dollhouse was hinged and could be closed and latched so that it could be carried like a suitcase.

"I'd like you to have it," Miss Anna said.

"But I... I couldn't..."

"Yes, you can, and you will," she said. "I know you are too old for playing with dolls, but I want someone to have this who will appreciate it. I just can't bear the thought of this dollhouse ending up in some ridiculous estate sale. Consider it a graduation present."

I didn't know what to say. It was a beautiful thing, and I could see how much it meant to her.

"It would be a great blessing for me, just knowing that you have it."

There was a handle on the peak of the roof, and I lifted the little house and carried it down the stairs, making sure of my footing so I would not drop it. As I walked with the bulky dollhouse, I noticed something silver dangling from one side.

Back in the kitchen, I sat the doll house next to the back door. I reached for the thing I had seen dangling off the side. I bent down to examine it.

It was a silver medallion on a fine silver chain. It was shaped like half a heart—the kind that is made to match another, where the two halves fit together to form a full heart. The half I held said *Sisters* on it. The chain had been caught in the hinge.

I opened the back of the dollhouse and freed the chain.

"Miss Anna," I said. I held up the chain and medallion. "I found this hanging on the dollhouse."

Miss Anna reached for it, placing the medallion in her palm. "I lost my half of the medallion. I was sick to death over it. Lost it playing in the house somewhere, and never did find it." She held the necklace to her breast. "I cried for weeks after losing it. With my half gone, my sister kept hers in the dollhouse. She didn't feel right wearing hers while mine was lost."

She put the medallion back in the dollhouse. "It belongs here…"

"Have another cookie, Hadlee," she said.

I did. They were always very good. Mom never took time to bake things, and I had never learned how.

"Will you teach me to bake cookies?" I asked.

Miss Anna raised an eyebrow. I don't think either of us had ever thought of baking cookies together before that day.

For the rest of that morning, Miss Anna and I baked a batch of chocolate chip cookies and talked about the old days.

Chapter 4

As I went out Miss Anna's back door carrying the dollhouse, I would have sworn she was about to cry. I felt awful taking the dollhouse, but at the same time, I felt honored that she wanted me to have it. I felt ready to cry myself.

I put the little dollhouse in my room, opened it up and examined the dolls and the furnishings. It was hard to believe that Miss Anna would part with it, but I understood. She was getting old and wanted to know it would be loved the way she loved it.

I discovered a number of details that I had not seen before. Tiny cloth curtains adorned each little window. The little doors dividing the rooms actually swung and had miniscule doorknobs made of glass beads. In the living room, on an end table, laid a black, Holy Bible with a teeny gold cross painted on the cover.

The detail overwhelmed me as I studied it. The hours it must have taken to produce this thing staggered me. I began to think of stories about its origins—perhaps an unmentioned but loveable old grandfather spent his retirement making these wonderful doll houses for adoring little granddaughters. All I knew was that I had fallen in love with it and would cherish it for as long as I lived. I hoped that maybe someday, I would have a young girl that I could pass it on to, so it could be loved forever.

I took out the dolls and examined them closely. They were made of cream-colored porcelain, the faces hand-painted. Both had painted gold hair. They were identical but for the color of the silk dresses. Amazing, diminutive works of art like I had never seen, being a child born in the age of plastics.

I rearranged the furniture and put both little Anna and Emma in a shared bedroom, just like it had been in real life.

I did not want to try therapy again. I didn't feel it would work for me, but Mom wanted to see me do *something*. I spent the rest of the day researching some treatment options online. Willow River was such a small town that there was nothing available there, so I had to look for something in nearby Freeport or Rockford. I had never gotten a driver's license, so I would have to depend on Dad to take me, which would be a real pain for him, but he would do it if I wanted to go.

We had tried it before, and it turned out to be a really bad idea. I got so anxious and frustrated within minutes and had to leave or risk having a full-out panic attack in front of all those people. It was one of the scariest things I had ever done, but I had been willing to try.

I once found a counselor who was willing to chat with me online, which is something I can tolerate quite well. But after a few sessions, she insisted that we needed to meet in person, claiming that the online sessions could only be used as the ice-breaker, and that she needed to be face-to-face to really be able to help. But she was physically located in Chicago, too far away to be a real treatment option.

"Whatcha doing?" Dad asked from my doorway. I had not heard him approach.

"Research," I replied.

"Oh."

He knew what research meant. It wasn't the first time Mom had set a deadline, and after all, Mom was a doer.

"I figured your graduation would set off another round of this," Dad said.

I didn't reply.

"You know she just wants to see you get better. She wants to see you make some progress, make an attempt."

"I know, and I wish it were that easy."

I felt his hands on my shoulders.

"Mom and I are not going to be around forever you know… hey, what's this?"

I turned to find him looking at the dollhouse.

"Miss Anna gave it to me."

"It would bring a good price on eBay," he said. "You don't see something like this every day."

I spun in my chair. "Don't even say that!" I spat, a little more harshly than intended. "It was hard for her to part with, and it meant a lot to her that I have it."

"Whoa, I was just kidding." He held up his hands in a sign of surrender.

I turned back to my computer.

"I did a little research for you," Dad said. "I found something you might consider. Sounds like it would be right up your alley."

"Really?"

"Really. I'll send you the link and you can check it out."

"Thanks," I said. I stood and gave him a hug.

"We're on our own for dinner tonight," he said. "Mom texted me and said she had a late showing. There's chili in the fridge. Let me know when you want…"

"I'll warm it up and call you," I said. "Right after *Star Trek* is over."

He smiled and waved his hand. "That's my girl."

***

Dad and I ate chili on TV trays in his den. Mom hated it when we did that, but we made sure to clean up, and what she didn't know…

I was tired and told Dad goodnight, asking him to tell Mom goodnight for me. Dad had brought home a box of used paperbacks from a rummage sale, and I spied one that I wanted to get started on called *Ender's Game*. It sounded really good, and Dad highly recommended it.

I got to my room and turned on the light, which had been working normally since Dad looked at it the night before. I put the book on my nightstand and pulled my sweatshirt over my head. With my arms still entangled in the sleeves, I looked at the dollhouse and saw something odd.

Both of the dolls had been moved. I remembered putting them in the same room, just like little Anna and Emma when they were young and inseparable, and now they were at opposite ends of the little dollhouse.

They were also both upside-down.

The dolls were standing on their heads, their bodies leaning into a corner to keep them in their inverted position. Their faces were in the corners.

That creepy chill rushed over me, just like it had the night before.

I took deep breaths to calm myself and began to think.

Dad had not come to my room since he had first seen the dollhouse earlier in the afternoon. I didn't remember him touching it at all. Even if he did, why would he have separated the dolls and turned them upside-down?

Lizzy could not possibly be responsible. While I could see her pawing and playing with the contents of the dollhouse, there was no way she could have positioned the dolls as I had found them. Lizzy stared at me from the doorway, looking innocent.

I stared at the dolls, hoping to think of a reasonable answer as to how this had come about.

But there was no answer.

I had put them together, representing the love of the young twin sisters, just like in Miss Anna's stories.

My mind was warped, but not that warped. I reached into the dollhouse and stood the dolls back on their feet, back in the same room. I did that just to remember that I did it, and to know for sure that I left it that way.

I grabbed the paperback and began reading the words, even though none of them were sinking in. My mind was on the dollhouse and the twin porcelain dolls.

Chapter 5

I had to admit it; there was only one thing I could think of to explain the dolls.

But I had lived in this house most of my life and had never experienced anything that even remotely made me think *ghost*.

Nothing else happened that day, or the next.

Just as I was about over the weirdness of the inverted dolls and my nerves had gone back to normal, things began to happen again that convinced me my home was indeed haunted.

It was two days after the inverted doll episode. I remember it well, because I was in my room visiting a new website for online group therapy. I was actually somewhat excited about it. It was the site that my dad discovered, and he had sent me a link in my email.

It was a new approach to group therapy for those like me with anxiety issues. You started out with just the counselor in a private forum, and when you felt comfortable with that arrangement, you were elevated to a group forum. The group consisted of those who had chosen to move past the one-on-one sessions. After a while, when you felt you were ready, you could move to live Skype sessions, where everyone was face-to-face through cameras on their computers.

As you got more comfortable with the forum members, you could choose to meet in real life at participating centers, where you only meet with those you had met online.

It was a gradual immersion therapy group and seemed like something that would align with my perceived abilities. It was a way to build an extended family, and hopefully break down some of the anxiety barriers along the way.

Dad was correct; it was something right up my alley. I was excited to have the chance to see how far I could go. If I got nervous, the exit was just one click away.

The only holdback was the cost. Dad had not researched enough to find out the cost, and when I saw the price, I was taken aback. Yes, they had to hire counselors and set up the network, but this was the Twenty-First Century after all, so how could it cost over two-hundred dollars a month?

I was determined to find a way.

It was almost nine o'clock when I heard Mom come in that night. It seemed she was working later than usual recently, and now coming in at this hour seemed almost normal. She said she had been doing more of her paperwork in the office where she had access to copy machines and scanners and better computers than what we had at home.

I had eaten dinner a couple of hours earlier, so I wanted to go to bed after saying hi to Mom and telling her about the therapy group I had found. I wanted to see what she thought about the cost, and if there was any way we could afford it.

I found Mom in the kitchen, stacking a bunch of folders full of papers on the corner of the table. She turned when she heard my footsteps.

"So now I have to do dishes at nine o'clock after I put in a long day at work?" Those were the first words out of her mouth.

Dad must have made something, leaving some dirty dishes on the stove and counter.

"I'll do them now," I said, hoping to quell her foul mood.

"Good idea," she said. "The least you and your father can do is to clean up after yourselves."

I ran a sink of soapy water while Mom warmed up something in the microwave. I was nearly done when Mom dropped a Tupperware container into the sink.

"I'm not staying up," she said. "I'm beat."

"Mom?" I called as she started down the hall to her room. "Can I tell you about something?"

"If you can make it quick," she said. She stood in the doorway, waiting.

"I found a really promising therapy group," I said. "It sounds like something I could really get into and make work."

"Great," she replied, without any enthusiasm. "Tell me about it tomorrow. I'll be home early."

She walked to her room, the floors squeaking with each step. I heard the door close.

I dried and put away the dishes, then went to tell Dad goodnight.

Dad was on his computer when I walked into his den. He must not have heard me approach over the sound of the TV, because when he realized I was there, he quickly closed the window he was working in. He seemed a bit nervous though he pretended not to be.

"What's up?" he asked as he turned from his screen.

"I'm just heading off to bed," I said. "Mom's in a foul mood... just so you know."

He nodded, then looked into my eyes. He looked pale and tired. Dark bags sagged below his glassy eyes.

"Did you take your medicine tonight?" I asked.

He smiled. "Yes, Mommy."

"All of them?"

"I guess so..."

Mom had been on a rampage lately when she found out Dad sometimes missed his medicine.

I gave him a hug. His skin felt cold and clammy.

"Did you tell Mom about the online therapy?"

"I mentioned it. She was too tired to talk about it."

"I think I found a way to pay for it," he said. "If she says we can't afford it, you come talk to me."

"Okay," I said, dragging the word out. "Did you rob a bank or something?"

He grinned, but it was an odd grin.

"I made some headway with my business," he said. "I might have enough to keep you going for a while."

"Thanks, Dad," I said. I kissed his forehead.

I took a step toward the door and heard a crash behind me. Dad and I both jumped when his glass of iced tea hit the floor and shattered. My heart was still pounding as we stared at each other. The glass had been on a small table next to his computer. Neither of us was within three feet of it when it fell.

The look on his face made me laugh. I couldn't control myself. He looked so dumbfounded.

"Scared the crap out of me!" he said. He began chuckling too. He bent over to pick up the shards, and then leaned against the arm of his chair. He took a deep, noisy breath.

"You okay?"

"Just got a little dizzy," he said. He spun his chair and sat heavily, still pulling deep breaths.

I picked up the large shards and went to the kitchen for some towels. I hurried back; concerned that Dad should not be left alone until I knew he was all right.

I returned to the den with towels and a plastic grocery bag to put the remaining broken glass into. Dad was still sitting, staring blankly at the TV. His breathing had evened out to a steady pace. I sat with him for a while longer with an episode of *Warehouse 13* playing, but Dad was not paying much attention to it. His mind was definitely elsewhere at the time.

Lizzy sneaked into the room, following a path along the walls like cats tend to do, until she seated herself at my feet. She stared up at me, hunched, then leapt onto my lap. After kneading my lap to make it suitable for snuggling, she curled into a furry, purring, ball.

Dad had moved to the couch, stretched out and was now lightly snoring. I looked upon him and noted how his belly had gotten bigger while the doctors urged him to lose weight. Mom had nagged him about his unhealthy eating habits, but more recently had grown quiet about it.

Lizzy awoke with a start, looking around the room as if she was disoriented. She stood on my lap, tensed as if ready to jump. Her eyes eventually locked on something in the far corner of the room. I tracked her eyes, trying to see what had her attention. There was nothing in that corner except an old chair with a stack of magazines on the seat.

Lizzy hissed before she jumped down and scurried from the room. I wondered if cats had dreams, and if she might be reacting to something she had only dreamed about. I stared at that corner, telling myself that cats were weird anyway, and that I should chalk this up as odd cat behavior.

As I stood to turn off the light and go to my own room, something moved in that same corner. I only caught it from the corner of my eye, but there was a shape… a dark shape that shifted. I stared intensely and saw nothing, just the stack of magazines on the chair. That creepy chill climbed my spine again. I no longer wanted to turn off the light, so I was frozen, standing next to the switch, my heart beginning to beat faster.

I thought I was being silly. I forced myself to flip the switch off, and when I did, I was staring into that corner again. The room went dark, but light from the hallway filtered in, casting shadows on the wall behind the chair. Again, from the corner of my eye, the shadows shifted. Something moved, but when I focused on where the movement occurred, everything was still.

I looked over to Dad who had rolled onto his side and was breathing normally. The hair on my arms was standing now, my heart and mind racing at a feverish clip. I stood there, trying to focus on movement—any movement, when I felt a cool breeze brush past me. It was as if a window had been opened and the cold night breeze invaded the house, rippling my hair and kissing my cheek.

By then, I was in the throes of a panic attack. I felt pressure on my face and in my eyes, a headache began to build, and I had to focus on my breathing. I gave a last glance at Dad, still lying peacefully on the couch, oblivious to what I had just experienced.

I fled down the hall, seeking the refuge of my own room, where a thousand thoughts battled to reach the forefront of my mind. I closed the old squeaky door, thinking that I could keep whatever was in my house from entering my space. I climbed into my bed with my clothes on, thinking that I may still have to flee some dark presence. I worried about Dad, being on the couch in the very room where something lurked in the darkness.

I wanted to go to him, to sit beside him and ward off anything that might bring him harm. But there I laid, covers pulled up to my eyes, paralyzed and frantic, wondering how long until morning would come.

I glanced at the digital clock on my nightstand. The red, glowing digits spelled out 12:07 AM. Sunrise was still hours away, and I knew that I would not sleep that night. I was torn between the urge to go back to Dad's den, and just hunkering down where I was, where for the moment, I felt safe and warm.

I swear, I saw each and every minute tick by on my clock that night, hoping and praying for the sun to rise and evict the shadows from my room. It was the shadows that scared me; the shadows that moved and stirred cold air.

Chapter 6

Sunrise came just before seven o'clock late in March. As my room grew brighter, I felt more tired. Nothing more had happened during the night, and by sunrise, my eyes were so heavy it was difficult to keep them open.

Just as I was dozing off, I heard my mom literally scream my name.

"Hadlee! Come here now!"

I shot out of bed before I could think. As I raced down the hall, I wondered if the shadow-creature could still be in the house. Had Mom seen something?

I turned the corner into the kitchen to see Mom staring at me, red-faced with her hair in a tangled mess. She was wearing her robe and fuzzy slippers. She waved her arm as I stood there.

"Look at this," she said.

There were papers all over the floor. There must have been dozens of pages scattered around the table and on the seats of the chairs. Yellow papers and white papers, and a few that were pink.

"What happened?" was all I could say.

"What happened? Your damn cat is what happened," she said.

I heard the floor squeak behind me, and then felt Dad's hand on my shoulder.

I turned to him, looking for an ally.

"What's going on?" he said. He stepped over the papers and came closer to the table.

"Your daughter's cat apparently had a good time during the night," Mom said. "There are contracts here that I need for later this morning."

Mom started picking up the pages, looking at them and trying to put them back into some kind of order.

I started to pick up pages as well, not knowing how to help reassemble them into any kind of order.

"You think Lizzy did this?" Dad said.

Mom straightened up. "Who else could have done it?" Her voice was shaky. She was on the threshold of tears. "The cat has to go," Mom said. "I can't live like this. It will take me hours to put this back together, and I have a closing at eleven this morning."

I dropped to my knees and began gathering papers. I handed the stacks to Dad and he put them on the table.

Mom began to tell us that she had to find a particular contract and get those papers in order for her closing. The contracts had pre-printed numbers on each page, so we had to sort them based on that number, and then Mom would have to put them into specific order.

We all worked silently, with Mom emitting a sob now and then. I felt so bad for her. Lizzy had never done anything like this before. The worst thing she had ever done was to claw the corner of our dusty old couch. Occasionally, she dug some dirt out of the few potted plants in the house.

Mom shuffled papers, searching through the stacks that Dad and I were feeding her, assembling them into different groups, but concentrating on the one she needed later that morning.

"I'm still missing page 9 of 13 for this contract," Mom said. "It's about *Contingencies* and has the address on the bottom of the page."

Dad and I started looking for that particular page in the stacks of papers in front of us.

After a few minutes of shuffling, Dad said, "It's not in my stack."

I finished looking through my stack, and I also didn't find it.

"Great," Mom said. "I can't go back to the clients now and do it over. It has to be here."

Dad and I swapped stacks and went through them again.

"They were all paper clipped," Mom said. "They should be close together."

I stood up, thinking that a page might have drifted away when they fell. I started searching behind things and found nothing.

"If they were paper clipped, do you think Lizzy took off the paper clips and then scattered the pages like this?" Dad said.

"Paperclips can come off," Mom said, "especially when a whole stack hits the floor at once."

I went to the counter to get a glass for a drink of water. I turned on the tap and noticed a sheet of paper on the counter that looked like what we had been sorting.

"Here's a page, way over here," I said. It wasn't the one we were searching for, but I added it to the stack.

"If Lizzy pushed the stack off the table, how does a page end up on the counter, more than eight feet away?" Dad was looking at me.

I shrugged my shoulders. I was so tired I could barely think straight.

Dad stood up and walked to the counter. Then he found a page on top of the microwave. He held it up and rattled it to get our attention.

"On top of the microwave?" he asked, rhetorically.

Mom paid no attention, but I saw his point.

Dad continued searching, walking toward the refrigerator. He pulled open a drawer and retrieved a flashlight. I saw him look between the fridge and the counter, thinking a page could have fallen between them. He stood up and looked on top of the fridge. He pulled down a sheet of paper and looked at it.

"Page 9 of 13," he said. "It's titled, *Contingencies*." He raised an eyebrow as he looked at me. "So how does Lizzy scatter these papers in a way that one lands on top of the refrigerator?"

Mom still wasn't paying much attention, but she took the page from Dad and added it in the proper order, as if nothing out of the ordinary had happened.

Dad looked at me and raised his hands in an *I give up* gesture.

Lizzy had not done this. There was no way that she could have separated all those pages, removed the paperclips, and placed some of the pages on top of the microwave or refrigerator.

My mind went right to the shadows I saw the night before. The fear began to claim me again. I had never experienced anything like this before, and up until now I had not believed in spooks. Even then, I was still not convinced it wasn't just an odd coincidence. Perhaps Mom or Dad were sleepwalking during the night? Maybe one of them opened a window or door that blew the papers around in such an odd fashion? I read a lot of science fiction, and had a hard time convincing myself that something of a paranormal nature was going on in my house.

But later that night, I became convinced that a supernatural phenomenon was happening on Tangled Trail.

Chapter 7

Mom made it to her meeting with a complete contract while Dad and I put the remaining papers in order at the kitchen table. We were both quiet at first, and I believe we were both thinking the same things, even though neither of us wanted to admit it.

"Could have been a downdraft from the chimney," Dad said, but sounded unconvinced. There was an old fireplace between the kitchen and dining rooms, a throwback from a bygone era that had not been used in my lifetime. Dad got up and walked over to it, pulling an old metal lever to one side of the mantle.

"Damper is closed," he said. There was a stack of newspapers on one side of the hearth, undisturbed. "And these papers would have been tossed around too." He took his seat and began sorting papers again.

"I know that Lizzy didn't do it," I said. Then I realized that I had not seen Lizzy since the night before. It was my turn to take a break.

I went to my room first, since that was Lizzy's favorite napping place. She loved to curl up on my bed when the morning sun beat in through my solitary window.

She wasn't in my room, and it didn't look like she had eaten any food since I fed her at dinner the night before. I checked Dad's den, Mom's bedroom and the living room. The upstairs was still blocked off as we awaited spring. Dad always closed the doors to both sets of stairs, then laid a sheet of foam insulation across the opening at the top of the stairs to help stop any cold drafts.

34

The door to what we called the back stairway was open slightly, the strike plate having been missing for as long as I remember. The door opened with a groan, and I looked up the worn, wooden steps. The light foam insulation sheet was still in place. Could Lizzy have pushed beneath it and gone beyond?

The back stairway was seldomly used. The old, light blue paint was peeling and falling on the stairs in curled chips. I brushed aside some cobwebs and made my way to the top. A wave of cool air drifted past me as I pushed the foam out of the way. I walked down the dusty hallway, softly calling for Lizzy. It was quiet, and dust motes floated on the drafts.

I went to my summer room first, because Lizzy stayed with me when I slept there. A single, bare bedframe stood along the wall. The mattress had been moved to my winter room back in October. Lizzy was nowhere in sight, but I noticed the closet door was slightly ajar, so I peeked inside. Some old clothes still hung in the closet, and a cardboard box lay on its side on the floor. I nudged it with my foot to see if it was empty.

It wasn't.

I heard a faint mewl, so I bent down and turned the box so the open side was toward me. Lizzy looked at me, stretched, then climbed out of the box.

I snatched her into my arms, cuddling and nuzzling her as I always did. She responded normally, nudging me and encouraging the continued attention.

"What are you doing up here?" I asked. "Let's get back downstairs where it's warmer. You must be starving."

As I made my way back to the stairs, Lizzy began to fidget. As I stood looking down the stairs, Lizzy went berserk. Her front claws sunk into my shoulder, while her back claws tried to climb my chest. She twisted and turned in my grasp until I lost my grip on her. She jumped to the floor with a thud and scurried back toward my summer room.

I looked back down the stairs. There was nothing scary there—at least that I could see. It was obvious that Lizzy didn't want to return to the first floor, and I wondered why.

I returned to my room, looked in the box and saw that Lizzy had climbed back inside. But she wasn't curled up and taking a nap. She faced the opening of the box, poised as if to defend it. Her front claws were bared, her eyes cautious.

I reached in to pet her, and she retreated deeper into the box.

"Fine," I said and turned away.

I fetched her food and water dish, placing them at the top of the stairs in case she got hungry.

After returning to the kitchen table, I was rubbing my shoulder. Dad had finished sorting the remaining papers, and he gave me a glance.

"You find Lizzy?"

"She's upstairs and doesn't want to come back down. I've got the scars to prove it."

I sat back down, dead tired and hungry.

"We're still missing one page," Dad said as he tidied the stack. "Page 7 of 12 is still missing. It's part of a deed abstract."

"I'll look around some more," I said. "Could it be behind the stove or refrigerator?

"Who knows?" He took a sip of his coffee. "There's blood on your shirt."

I glanced at my shoulder. Not only were there a few spots of blood, but the material was snagged where Lizzy's claws had dug in.

"She's never done that before," I said in Lizzy's defense.

I put two slices of bread in the toaster. "So, what do you think happened in here?" I asked.

Dad shook his head. He looked at me with a lost expression on his face. "I honestly have no idea."

I wanted to say our house was haunted, but also didn't want to cross a line I could not step back over. As if saying it would make it real.

"But I agree that it wasn't Lizzy," he said. "No way did she scatter these papers like that."

I buttered my toast while it was hot, then opened the fridge to get the strawberry jelly. I was starved, and asleep on my feet. I put the jelly on my toast, opened the fridge and before I put the jar on the shelf, I spied a sheet of paper between the gallon of milk and the orange juice. I pulled it out and looked it over.

Title Abstract—page 7 of 12.

I carried it to Dad.

"This was in the refrigerator," I said, "on the top shelf."

He looked at me, dumbfounded.

"I was on the couch all night," he said. "I didn't dream, and only woke up once to go pee." He looked at me hard. "What about you?"

"I was awake all night," I said. "I couldn't sleep."

I didn't want to mention the shadows in his den and the cold air that chilled me to the core.

"Your mom hasn't seemed right, lately," Dad said. "I'm kind of worried about her. She seems a bit distant… and…" He hesitated, searching for a word. "Scatterbrained."

"You think Mom did this?"

"I don't know. What do you think?"

"I don't know either," I said. "You think she could be having a breakdown or something?"

Dad just shook his head.

I ate my toast, and like a zombie, staggered to my room. I flopped onto the bed and burrowed under the blankets. I wanted Lizzy to climb onto the bed to keep me company. I needed sleep and felt like I might be able to sleep as long as the sun was shining.

I dreaded the coming of nightfall.

Chapter 8

I know I managed to sleep for a while, because I had dreams. I dreamed that I was a little girl again, and Miss Anna and her twin Emma, were also little girls at the same time. We all lived in the same house—the house I live in now.

Little Anna and Emma wore the prettiest dresses; one in yellow, one in green. They wore shiny white shoes with a single strap and silver buckle. The house was beautifully painted yellow and green, with white trim. The sidewalks were perfectly flat and new, not the crumbling and broken walks that I knew.

Emma and Anna whispered into each other's ears a lot, cupping a hand to keep me from overhearing. They finished each other's sentences, told each other jokes, and giggled in the same way. In the dream we were having fun.

Then the sky darkened as a storm approached. The leaves started blowing off the trees as they danced in the wind. Lightning struck in the distance, and then the twins were gone. The last thing I remember from the dream was running down the basement stairs. When I got to the dark basement, I could hear the twins crying. I woke up before I found them.

The dream made me think of Miss Anna, and I wanted to talk with her. She was always so gentle and understanding. I had something I wanted to ask her; something that I didn't want my parents to know about just yet.

My digital alarm clock read 5:07 PM, so I thought I would see what Dad was up to before doing a little research online.

Dad was napping on his couch. I left him be and went back to my room.

I sat at my computer and did a search for hauntings and ghosts. I had never considered ghosts much before that time, but in light of recent events I wanted to know more. I had seen the TV shows where groups of people went to a supposedly haunted house and set up cameras and audio recorders, sometimes capturing a strange sound and sometimes a strange image. But to me, it was hard to call those findings evidence of ghosts.

I hit many websites and read a good number of articles that described hauntings. At that point, I had convinced myself that the strange occurrences I'd experienced in the past few days had to be my imagination getting the best of me, in the same way that the creaking door sounded much more ominous after watching a scary movie. I may have just primed myself to watch for things that didn't really exist—except in my broken mind.

But then there were the papers... How do I explain that?

I needed to at least acknowledge the possibility that we might have a ghost in the house.

I glanced out the window and saw Miss Anna walking back from her mailbox. I hurried out the door pulling on my sweater as I went.

She saw me coming and stopped where the sidewalk diverged to each of our houses.

The sun was low in the west and a chilly breeze was blowing in from the north. Miss Anna pulled her jacket tightly around her as she held her mail. She smiled at me like she always did.

"How are you, my dear?"

"I'm okay," I said. "Do you have any cookies?"

Asking for cookies was a code between us that meant I would like to chat for a while.

"Of course," she said. "I still have some of the snickerdoodle cookies we made a few days ago." She wrapped an arm around me and we talked about the weather and the coming of spring as we walked to her back door. Miss Anna pointed out some tulips emerging from the cold soil on the south side of her house.

I placed paper plates and napkins on the table while Miss Anna took a container of cookies out of her cupboard. "I have cherry Kool-Aid today," Miss Anna said.

I nodded my approval. Miss Anna seemed to really enjoy serving me cookies and Kool-Aid. I think she just enjoyed having someone over to talk to.

Miss Anna had no living relatives. She had a few friends, but it was rare for her to have visitors. Like me, she rarely left her house.

Miss Anna's lonely life made me think that someday, I might find myself in her shoes. Like Miss Anna, I had no siblings. My mom was an only child whose parents died before I was born. My dad had a sister who lived in upstate New York. She had never married and hadn't come to visit in years. Those thoughts made me glad that I could visit with Miss Anna, and I truly did look forward to talking with someone other than my parents.

I took a sip of my Kool-Aid and listened to Miss Anna tell about her desire to plant some new flowers and tend to her garden in the coming weeks. For a woman in her eighties, Miss Anna was still pretty active around her house. While she hired handymen to paint the house, fix windows and perform other maintenance needs, she tended to her yard work herself. She had a petite build and wore brightly-colored floppy hats and gloves when she worked outside. I sometimes watched her pull weeds and rake leaves for hours at a time.

I sat at the table, working in my mind to determine the best way to frame my question. It just sounded so strange and was a topic I was not yet comfortable with, but I had a nagging desire to get the question out.

It must have shown on my face.

"I can tell you are dying to ask me something, Hadlee."

I finished chewing and washed it down with the red Kool-Aid.

I looked into Miss Anna's old weepy eyes. "Do you believe in ghosts?"

I could see the surprise on her face, but it lasted only a moment. She studied me; now her own mind searching for answers. Her answer said more than the actual words spoken.

"Why do you ask?"

I shrugged and tried to make it seem as if I was only asking a stupid question and not something that I was really curious about. Miss Anna could read my face as if it were a billboard.

"Has something happened?"

I shrugged again. "Just some things moved around in the house. Some things we found that were not where we left them." I was trying to be cool about it, and I think I failed.

Miss Anna nodded and studied me some more. I wondered what my face was telling her now.

"It scared you," she said. "Whatever happened, scared you, and now you are looking for explanations."

I nodded and took a quick bite of my cookie. I didn't know how to carry on this conversation now that I had started it.

Miss Anna scooted her chair closer to mine and took my hand. "Tell me what happened," she said. "I can tell something has disturbed you deeply."

I told her about Mom's papers being scattered around the kitchen, and how she had blamed Lizzy and wanted the cat out of the house. I told her there was no way Lizzy was the culprit.

Miss Anna smiled. A comforting, easy smile that did not judge or condemn, but simply said she understood.

Miss Anna offered some of the same explanations that Dad offered, focused on a sudden gust of wind from an unknown source. I countered every argument with cold logic.

"Perhaps it was a combination of things," Miss Anna offered. "Maybe Lizzy did knock over the stack of papers, but then a downdraft from the chimney or an open door sent them flying."

I knew that what scattered the papers was something we had yet to discover.

"You want to protect Lizzy," Miss Anna said. "So, you are looking for any kind of explanation that would render Lizzy innocent. That seems like a natural response to me."

I didn't tell her about the paper I found inside the refrigerator, and I still wanted an answer to my original question.

"Do you believe in ghosts?"

Miss Anna took only a second to reply. "No," she said. "I don't believe in ghosts." She was shaking her head and she avoided my eyes. She scooted her chair back to its original position. "I think the idea of ghosts is a silly one." She stood up and went to the sink to rinse out her glass. "I believe that when people die, they stay dead."

Her words had a tone several degrees cooler than they had just a moment before.

She turned back to me, looking rather stern. "I believe when people die, they are taken from us forever," she said. "And I believe that's how it should be."

I could tell that Miss Anna had no more to say on the subject. She then became her sweet self again and invited me to look at the tulips she spotted on the way into the house.

Chapter 9

I left Miss Anna when I saw my dad walking out the back door of our house. He glanced around and spotted me.

"There you are," he said. "I've been looking for you."

He put his arm around me as he led me toward the garage. "I'm going to a place in Freeport," he said. "They have some inventory that I might pick up for pennies on the dollar." He did a fist-pump and said, "cha-ching!"

He kissed me on the forehead.

"Your mom texted me, saying she might be late. You're on your own for dinner. I saw some leftover chicken in the fridge."

"Okay," I said. "I have some things to do anyway."

He was walking away from me, but suddenly turned around. "Oh," he said. "I meant to tell you something."

He came back and stood before me on the sidewalk.

"Have you talked to your mom about the online therapy group we found?"

"I tried to," I said. "She didn't have time."

"Okay," Dad said. "I can pay for the first three months. Let's not even mention it to Mom."

This was totally out of character for Dad. "Okay," I said, a bit dumbfounded. "Are you sure?"

"Yeah," he said. "I made some good sales lately, and if we just pay for three months, we will know whether you think it's worth continuing. We can tell your mom at that point."

I just stood there, sorting out how I felt about it.

"It will be fine," Dad said. "This money is a windfall. I sold some stuff that I basically got for nothing, and I want you to try out this new therapy group. I think it could be just the ticket we've been looking for."

I nodded, thinking $600 is a lot of money in the Monroe household, and knowing Mom would have plenty to say about it. But I also understood that Mom might just nix the whole thing without much thought. Like Dad, I thought this online therapy might be perfect for me.

"It's our secret," he said. "I'll pay for three months later tonight when I get home."

I gave him a big hug, suddenly feeling optimistic.

"Thanks, Dad." I kissed his cheek.

Dad got into his old Jeep Cherokee and I watched as he disappeared down Tangled Trail.

I first went to check on Lizzy, who I found at the top of the stairs, seemingly ready to rejoin the household. I hoped Mom was not serious about banishing her from the house. After lifting the foam insulation to allow Lizzy access to the stairs, I reached for her food and water dish.

Lizzy slinked down the steps and rounded the corner into the kitchen before I made it down. I filled her dishes and went to my room. I looked at the dollhouse, admiring the details yet another time. The figurines were still in the upstairs room where I had left them, standing in their pretty green and yellow dresses, reminding me of my dream.

I pulled up my favorite search engine and started looking for websites about ghosts.

Ghosts were apparently big business, and I avoided the websites looking to sell things like books and DVD's. I found a few forums where regular people talked about ghosts, asking common questions and relating paranormal experiences.

Tangled Trail

It was easy to lose myself in those forums. The idea that so many people shared things that could only be explained by paranormal activities led me deeper and deeper into the theories, lore and mythology that surround hauntings.

My eyes were tired from reading the screen, and I looked away. The digital alarm clock said 7:13, but some of the LED segments were flickering. The clock normally displayed the digits in a steady red glow, but now the individual line segments grew brighter and weaker, as if the power was fluctuating.

The overhead light was steady, and my computer monitor seemed fine.

I stared at the clock, watching and hoping it was not about to die on me. I think Dad had picked it up at a yard sale a few years ago.

The numbers faded until the entire display was black. *Just my luck*, I thought. I really liked that clock.

Then the line segments began to show signs of life once again, some of them glowing stronger as if they were struggling to survive. After a few seconds, some of the lines glowed brightly again, and others remained dead. The display now simply read gibberish.

I thought of unplugging it to see if a reset would make any difference. Then I looked at the display once again and saw something that made my heart race. Instead of numbers, the individual LED elements spelled out a word. The display read:

LIES

Had that word not showed up on my computer screen a few nights before, I would have chalked it up to coincidence. In my bones I knew this was not just chance, but a message.

I was too astonished to think clearly. Too many thoughts tried to pass through the narrow funnel of coherent thought at one time. As I stared at the unblinking display, it began to flicker again. Some of the line segments started to pulse a weak red, then steadily grow brighter, like a heart struggling to pump precious blood. I blinked to clear the tears of bewilderment from my eyes.

All of the digits returned to normal, reading 7:15. It was then that a cool breeze brushed past me, tingling my nose and cheeks, cooling my throat and lungs as it passed. I turned, as if to follow whatever was moving past. Lizzy was just outside my door, eyes large and perceptive. She backed into the wall as she tried to turn. I heard her claws attempting to get traction on the bare wood floors in the hallway.

I could not believe what I just experienced. It was like so many of the stories I had read online where people claimed the presence of a ghost.

My breathing paused when I glanced at the dollhouse. The doll dressed in yellow was on the floor, directly under the table that held the miniature house. On top of the prone doll was a silk rose that had come from a vase on my windowsill. I glanced at the window and saw the vase there as usual, with five other silk roses still in it.

I checked myself over while sitting in my chair, as if to make sure I was still okay.

I didn't know what to do. It seemed to me that the ghost was trying to tell me something, perhaps warning me.

The word was LIES. I wracked my brain trying to remember if I had lied to someone recently. My circle of people was quite small; three to be exact. Maybe the lie wasn't intentional. Could I have told someone something that I only thought was true?

I had to leave my room. I decided to take a walk down Tangled Trail until I came to the highway, just a half-mile away. If Mom or Dad returned while I was out walking, I could hitch a ride back, saying I just wanted some fresh air.

Fresh air clears the mind.

At least that's what Miss Anna always said.

Chapter 10

What had just happened was well beyond the boundaries my mind had set for this world. I was numb. My emotions were just a jumbled mass of visceral thoughts. It was as if I could no longer rely on anything I believed.

There was a being in my house. A spirit, a haunt—whatever noun you want to assign to it—I seemed to have one.

Mom and Dad would not believe me unless there was some evidence that could not be explained in another way. Ghosts, as foreign as they were in my world, would be even more anomalous in theirs. I knew this, because I knew my parents.

Miss Anna did not believe in ghosts, but I wondered if there was just the slightest doubt in her mind. Of the three adults in my tiny universe, Miss Anna was the most open-minded.

I pondered my next move. My entire social existence was online, so that was where I had to seek answers. I could muster enough courage to reach out to someone who knew about these things; someone who could tell me if we were in any danger, or what we could do to keep the ghost away.

I made it to the end of Tangled Trail and stood by the side of the road for a few moments. The night breeze had a cutting edge to it, but I had worked up a sweat. A few cars passed on the highway leaving a blast of noise and exhaust fumes in their wake. The tall trees were still void of leaves, their skeletal remains swaying in the breeze.

I wanted to be back in my room, but not with the ghost. I thought back to the ceramic doll that had been on the floor, under the dollhouse with the silk rose lying across it. It did not seem to me that these were just random things. I tried to see the significance—if there was any—to an implied message.

LIES.

A thought hit me. Dad and I had just discussed not telling Mom about the online therapy and how Dad was going to pay for it out of some windfall profit he had made. I believed that not divulging relevant information could be the same as lying. Not telling Mom about the cost of the class was the only thing I could think of that could be considered lying.

I sometimes told Mom her outfit looked great when it really didn't, or sometimes I would tell Dad that I liked a movie that I really didn't. Was that truly lying? Did the Universe really hold that high a moral code? More importantly... did the ghost?

It was getting colder as I stood by the side of the dark road, so I turned to walk back to the house.

My thoughts turned to Lizzy. She had fled my doorway, and I assume by her reactions that she could sense the ghost. She had reacted the same way in Dad's den the night I glimpsed the strange shadow.

I had often seen in movies and read in books that animals have the ability to sense things that we humans cannot. That seemed to be at least scientifically plausible. Animals could smell things and hear things far beyond the abilities of humans. Birds of Prey could see many times better than we humans. It seemed logical that cats might sense what we call paranormal activities.

I made it back to the house with my mind still on overload. There were signs of life at Miss Anna's house. I could see the flash of her TV through her curtains, which made me feel a little better knowing she was still up.

My heart began racing as I approached the back door. I had seen Poltergeist on cable and hoped nothing was levitating inside.

Everything was still, and in every way, normal. I glanced around, looking for Lizzy, but was not surprised that I didn't find her.

I went directly to my room and found everything as it was left. The doll was still on the floor, and the silk rose still lay across it. I picked up the rose, and placed it back in the dusty vase, thinking of it as an act of defiance. If the ghost was watching me at that moment, it probably laughed. I then retrieved the doll from the floor and put her back in the upstairs room with her sister.

I looked up to the ceiling. "Leave us alone," I said.

With my back against the wall, I waited for things to fly around or fall from shelves, but nothing happened.

I don't know what I expected, but I expected something.

***

I spent the next hour online, searching and reading. Everything I read about ghosts only added to my confusion. There were no articles with titles like "four easy steps to rid your house of ghosts". This was not science. What worked in one case may not work in another. There were no hard and fast rules concerning ghosts, and no two cases just alike.

I realized I was in over my head. I had to talk with someone, explaining what I had seen and felt, and see if I could get some honest suggestions on how to deal with it.

But therein lies my problem; I have extreme difficulties talking with real people.

I poured over some local ghost-hunter sites, only because someone local did not seem as intimidating as someone from far away. I know it's weird, but that is how I tend to apply my own logic to communicating when it's absolutely necessary.

I braced myself and began looking for names and email addresses. I found some and copied the hyperlinks. While I searched, one name seemed to appear more often than any others. There was apparently a person who others claimed could communicate with ghosts. Her name was Mary O'Reilly.

The threads I read about Mary were fascinating. Mary could (allegedly) communicate with ghosts on a level that nobody else could. She used her skills to help police solve mysteries, and also to help the ghosts themselves find peace and move on to other realms.

My dad had taught me to always apply the scientific method to problems. Systematic observation, measurement and experiment were how real problems get solved in the natural world.

But ghosts did not exist in the natural world. Ghosts were solidly in the world of the paranormal; the world that was unobservable, immeasurable and where experimenting might reveal more questions than answers.

I needed an expert on ghosts.

I searched the web for Mary O'Reilly and ghosts and turned up a few articles. I found out she lived in Freeport, which was only twenty miles or so from where I lived. I found an email address and copied the hyperlink into my email program.

Then I sat there a good while trying to figure out what to say. It all sounded so crazy when you tried to put it into words, and having other people think I was crazy went right to the crux of my anxiety issues.

I pushed away from the computer to give it some thought.

The back door in the kitchen opened with a creak and I heard my dad's heavy footsteps cross the kitchen floor. I met him in the hallway.

"Hey, kiddo."

He held a few small boxes in his arms and I followed him to his den.

Tangled Trail

It was almost 10 o'clock.

"When's Mom coming home?" I asked.

Dad pulled off his jacket and tossed it over a chair. "Anytime, I would think," he said.

He gave me a look and must have read something on my face.

"Why? What's going on?" he asked.

"Nothing," I lied, then immediately wondered if I would get another message from the ghost. I guess we lie more often than we realize. "It's just that it's late, and she's usually home by now." I sat heavily on Dad's couch. "Has she called you?"

"No. I haven't heard from her," he said. "She's probably just finishing up some paperwork at the office."

I saw a crazy set of shadows sweep the room, but it was just Mom's headlights turning into the driveway.

"There she is now," Dad said.

He slipped out of his shoes and walked toward the bathroom. I hated it when he peed with the door open and continued talking as he did so.

"I've got to get online and do some work," he shouted. "I got something good in the works."

"Good," I shouted.

When Dad said he had work to do, it was code for wanting to be left alone. I walked down the hall and met Mom coming in the back door.

She looked like a wreck. Her clothes were rumpled, and she carried more folders than anyone should ever attempt without a bag of some kind. I hurried over to take some of them.

"What a day," she said. She kicked off her shoes and took a seat, rubbing her feet.

"Did you get any dinner?" I asked, ready to offer to make her something.

"Yeah, I had a sandwich," she said with little enthusiasm. "I'm too tired to eat anyway. I'm just craving a warm bed."

She got herself a drink of water from the sink. "Tell your dad I'm going to bed. I'm exhausted."

I nodded. I wanted to give her a hug, but she had already turned away and wobbled down the hall.

I gave Dad the message, to which he barely shrugged. He was working on his computer and didn't look up.

I went to my room and closed the door behind me. I felt as though I could cry. I went to sit on my bed and realized Lizzy was curled up in her usual place. She stretched and yawned when I sat down beside her and began stroking her fur.

Things had changed in the Monroe house of late. Mom seemed more distant than ever, always working late and never saying much. She used to brush my hair, always commenting on how beautiful auburn-colored hair was, and suggesting I do something different with it. She said it was too pretty to always be in a ponytail. She often said that with my tall, slender build, I would someday drive the boys crazy. I think she said those things to try to entice me to go out into the big, wide world.

She had not even come into my room the past few days.

Dad seemed a little more preoccupied than before, looking pale and worn down. He seemed more sluggish than ever and complained of being tired a lot. He had always been a night-owl, but it seemed lately he napped throughout the day and night, and never really got in a lengthy sleep.

A thought occurred to me; could the ghost be affecting my family? Were Mom and Dad having experiences of their own, and like me, were just too afraid to say anything? It made me wonder if *I* had changed recently in their eyes. I felt more jumpy than usual, that was true. Could a ghost affect how my family interacted? After thinking about it, I rationalized that it certainly could. Nobody would be the same after experiencing the things I had seen.

I felt some action needed to be taken, so I pulled out my chair and opened a new email, addressed to Mary O'Reilly.

Dear Mary,

My name is Hadlee. I live in Willow River. We have a ghost in our house, and I'm really afraid of it.

Can you tell me how to get rid of this ghost? I've lived in this house most of my life, and we've never had a ghost here before.

I think my cat can see the ghost. She acts weird and runs away whenever the ghost is near.

I could really use some help. I hope you will email me.

Thank you,
Hadlee Monroe

It was hard for me to write that little note, as simple as it seems to most people. In my mind, I was convinced that Mary O'Reilly would think I'm a whacko and would laugh at me. It's ten times worse when trying to communicate with someone in person. My stomach twists and tightens, my face flushes and turns red. My head feels like an overinflated balloon. I start to stutter and can't put together a sentence, which makes it all the worse.

And it goes downhill from there.

Desperate, I hit the send button and hoped that I would get a reply soon.

The house was as quiet as a crypt. I glanced at my clock (it was working normally) and found it was after 11 PM. I was tired and wired—physically tired, but too wired to sleep. If I had known what was coming shortly after I sent the email to Mary O'Reilly, I may have held off, because I would have had a lot more to tell her.

Chapter 11

After reading more stories and articles about ghosts and hauntings, I left my room and walked as quietly as possible toward Dad's den. It was dark in his room, the only light emanating from various electronic devices scattered about his work area—each featuring a small LED light. Some blinked and others were steady, some red, some blue and others green or yellow. Those tiny lights set an eerie glow upon the room as I peeked inside.

Dad was on his couch, breathing noisily, each inhalation on the verge of a snore.

He had not slept in the bedroom with my mom for a few days now, which was another new development in the Monroe household that I took note of.

I crept down the hall to my mom's room. The door was only open a crack, revealing only darkness beyond. I listened for the sound of my mother's breathing. She coughed lightly. The bed springs squeaked as she rolled over, then all fell quiet once again.

I tip-toed back to my room. The glow of my computer screen lit the wall opposite my desk. Lizzy's eyes glowed faintly from the weak light as she watched me come into the room. She seemed relaxed, beckoning me to come to bed and snuggle with her.

I obliged, picking up my copy of *Ender's Game* and finding the place I had left off. Reading was my typical escape from reality when things got strange. I just wanted to lose myself in the story and grow sleepy to the point where I woke myself up by dropping the book on my face.

I turned on my small reading light and I buried myself in the blankets, looking for just the right position. Lizzy then had to resettle herself as well. The kitchen clock ticked distantly, faintly, a soothing sound sure to bring on sleep.

Just as I found myself struggling to stay awake, the wind made a strange moaning sound that echoed faintly through my room. I was half asleep when I first heard it, so I wasn't even sure I had not dreamed that sorrowful sound. I closed the book around my bookmark, and just lay there, staring up at the ceiling, focused on the soft wail. The wind was not blowing at that moment, and a quick glance out my window revealed the silhouette of the tall trees—all standing perfectly still against the cold, starry sky.

Then the sound came again, louder this time. Lizzy moved, but settled back into a soft, sleepy purr.

The sound was pitiful. A weeping groan that trailed off to nothing...then a gentle sigh. Logic said it had to be the wind playing around the gutters and downspouts, but I knew it was not. This sound contained emotion. Sadness or hatred, I could not determine, but it was so emotional as to bring tears to my eyes.

Again, the muted wail became louder, drawing my gaze to the closet.

Lizzy heard the sound and tried to burrow beneath me. Her head came up and glared at the closet, then she sunk into the blankets and emitted a whimpering mewl. The closet door stood between the bed and the hallway, and it was obvious to me that Lizzy would not chance passing it. I sat up in the bed. Lizzy got behind me, still trying to get under the blankets.

The sighs and moans continued, though muted. There was a slight echo to the sounds, as if someone cried into a large can.

My hands shook, and my blood pumped double time.

I stared at the closet as if I were a character in a movie. A battle was raging within me. Part of me wanted to run to my dad, and another part wanted to sooth some forlorn, suffering creature. I put my feet on the cold floor before I knew what I was about to do.

I stood, leaving Lizzy exposed on the bed. I looked at her as I stood there and saw the panic in her yellow eyes. She crouched as if to leap and run but stayed put as I turned back to the closet.

I stepped to the closet, the despairing sounds now becoming lost to my own heartbeat thrumming in my head. The arteries in my neck pulsed rapidly as I reached for the doorknob. I was vaguely aware that Lizzy shot past me and disappeared down the hall.

The closet door opened, and the cold air rushed over my face and my bare feet. My breath came out in a cloud. The sighing, crying sound continued, growing louder. I stared at the old pipes that went through the floor—the source of the painful sounds.

I leaned toward those pipes, so filled with sorrow that a sob escaped my trembling lips as a tear streaked down my face.

The sound stopped.

The hair on my arms stood erect as a chill coursed through me. It was as if some spell had been broken. The room was dimly lit by only my reading light. In the moment it took for me to find the switch for the ceiling light, darkness poured from the pipes like black smoke from a chimney. I shuddered, my fingers unable to flip the switch. A cold wind blew past me, sending my hair swirling and snatching the breath from my throat.

My fingers brushed the switch in the right direction and the glorious light filled the room. My hair fell over my face. The curtains on each side of the window still wavered as the shadows fled.

I was so shaken that I staggered back to my bed and sat, numb and cold.

It may have been a moment or an hour that I sat on the edge of my bed, my mind simply blank. Things like this just do not happen. It wasn't imagined, and I certainly was not dreaming this. It was then that I decided that I had to do something... but had no idea on how to proceed.

My thoughts turned to my dad. I walked quickly to his den and found him still sleeping on his couch, his breaths almost silent now.

I again crept to my mom's room, like a thief in a movie. No sounds from within.

Lizzy was gone, hiding somewhere in the big old house.

It was hard to go back in my room, but I had no place else to go, and no place that would offer exile from a restless spirit.

Mom and Dad never attended church, so neither had I. But on that night, I said a sincere prayer to God Almighty that he would protect us from whatever inhabited our house on Tangled Trail.

Chapter 12

After hours of sitting at my desk, pacing in my room, and thinking, I finally calmed down. There were no further signs of the ghost that night, and morning was just an hour away.

I lay down on my bed, resting my eyes and stretching my back. I was exhausted, but my mind was still whirling with possibilities. Let the scientific method be damned. There was a spook in our house, and that rocked my already precarious world.

I wanted to know what Mom and Dad knew about this. I needed to question them about it but be clever and not give away what I knew.

It wasn't long until I heard Dad go to the bathroom. He was noisy in almost everything he did, and his trips to the bathroom were no exception. He hacked up some phlegm, belched and then flushed. The pipes rattled and groaned as loud as Dad did.

I went to the kitchen and pretended to be reading the paper that was left on the table.

Dad walked in a moment later, scratching and stretching.

"I feel like crap," were his first words.

He looked like crap too. The bags under his eyes were two shades darker than the rest of his face, which was much paler than usual. His hair was all over the place, as if he had just walked through a hurricane. There were beads of sweat on his forehead and upper lip.

"What's wrong?"

He began shaking his head as he leaned on the back of a chair.

"I don't know," he said. "Maybe I have a touch of flu or something. I feel weak and…" He took a couple of deep breaths. "I feel wasted."

Dad wasn't in any kind of shape at all. He wasn't usually up this early, so I thought I might be seeing him how he would be if he did get up this early.

"I didn't sleep worth a damn," he said, still leaning on the chair. "I kept waking up every few minutes, even though I was tired as hell."

I saw an opening and tiptoed into it. "What kept you up?"

He pulled out the chair and sat down, putting his elbows on the table. "I don't know," he said. "I kept hearing noises at first, and then I dozed off and woke up with the chills."

Noises. Chills. I could relate.

Dad glanced over to the coffee pot which was on a timer. It had thirty minutes before it kicked in, and that was because it was set for Mom.

"Can you kick the coffeemaker on please?"

I did, and then sat again.

"What kind of noises did you hear last night?"

"I don't know," he said. "You know how this old house moans and groans. It must have been enough to wake me up, that's all I remember."

"Do you want me to make you something to eat?"

The look on his face said he wasn't hungry, but Dad rarely passed up food.

"Do we have any fruit and cream oatmeal?"

I got up to look. "Is peaches and cream okay?"

He nodded.

It was instant oatmeal, just sixty seconds to make.

Mom walked in before the timer went off. She walked directly to the coffee pot and saw that it was already going. "Who started the coffee?"

"Dad needed a cup," I said. "He's not feeling well."

She gave him a hard look. "Have you been taking your pills?"

"I've been taking them," Dad said weakly. "I take them every day."

"You haven't taken this morning's dose," she replied.

"I just got up," Dad said.

She gave him a cold stare. "Take your pills. I'm sure you will feel better." She placed the pill organizer in front of him.

Dad looked so tired, but he nodded and said he would take them with his coffee.

"Did you sleep well?" I asked my mom.

"I haven't slept well in a week," she said while staring at the coffee maker, as if willing it to hurry.

As I watched Mom, there was a clattering sound that startled me. I was sitting across the table from my dad and looked in the direction of the noise.

There were pills all over the floor, the organizer against the wall across the room.

"What the hell are you doing?" Mom shouted.

Dad stared back at her dumbly. "I didn't do anything," he said.

"If you don't want to take the goddamn pills, then don't take them!" Mom was angry. I think she woke up angry, and now she had a good excuse to let it out.

"I swear to God that I didn't do that!" Dad said. "I didn't touch it!"

I had been sitting right there and had not seen Dad move. While I wasn't looking directly at him, I'm sure I would have noticed a move like throwing the pills.

Dad looked at me. I could tell he was completely dumbfounded.

As Mom was staring at Dad, a cupboard above the fridge flew open. More pills scattered across the kitchen floor. Two plastic bottles rolled back and forth as we all just stared at each other in dismay.

"Where is that goddamn cat?" Mom shouted. She stomped around the kitchen as if looking for something to strangle.

"Lizzy's not even in here," I said. "She's been hiding."

Mom dropped to the floor and began scooping up the pills. "Things don't just fly out of the cupboard! Find that cat and make sure you put her outside. I'm done with that cat!"

Dad went to his knees and began helping Mom pick up the pills.

"Get out of my way, Blake," Mom said. "I'll do this."

I knew Lizzy had not done this—and even worse, I knew what did. I had been looking at Mom when the door cupboard flew open, and I saw those bottles being ejected as if by an invisible hand.

"Where are the lids?" Mom asked rhetorically as she looked around. She had a full bottle in her hand with no cap.

Dad and I shot up and began looking for the lids while Mom scooped the remaining pills off the floor. I went right to the cupboard and stood on my tippy-toes to look inside. On the only shelf in that cupboard, sat two plastic caps. I retrieved them, then handed them to Mom.

"They were still in the cupboard," I said.

Mom snatched the caps from my hand and screwed one on the full bottle. Dad went back to his chair. Neither of them seemed bothered by the fact that the lids were off before the bottles flew out of the cupboard. I don't think the significance of that fact registered with either of them.

I got weak and had to sit down. My world could only be rocked so many times before my mind would try rejecting what I had seen. My life had suddenly taken a turn that I never expected. My home, the only home I had ever known, was now a place of fear.

I needed to get out of the house. The only place I could go was next door. Miss Anna always rose early. I went to the back door and sat on a small bench to put on my shoes. I was deep in thought and didn't even tell Mom and Dad I was going out. I opened the door and saw a black shape dart past my feet.

Startled, I leaned against the doorframe and watched as Lizzy ran down the steps and across the back yard. I called to her, but she never looked back and disappeared around the corner of the house. I guess she wanted out of the house too, and for the same reason.

Chapter 13

I took the sidewalk to Miss Anna's house and knocked on her back door. Within a minute, she let me in with a look of surprise on her face.

"Hadlee? Sweetie, are you okay?"

"Not really," I said. "I needed to get out of the house."

Miss Anna gave me a sympathetic look and stood aside to let me in.

There had been many times in the past few years that I sought refuge at Miss Anna's house. Once I was old enough to be more independent, there were times when I had to get away from Mom or Dad to help me get a different perspective. Since Miss Anna's house was the only place I could really go, she seemed to understand and was always accommodating.

"Nothing serious, I hope," Miss Anna said as she closed the door.

I didn't know how to answer her. Yes, the situation was serious, but I just could not let myself burden Miss Anna with talk of ghosts. But I also wanted her input on the happenings next door. I wanted to know if she thought we were in any danger, or if she had any advice on what to do.

She had already told me she didn't believe in ghosts, but I now knew that ghosts exist. I wasn't looking for opinions, I was looking for solutions.

"I can make some Kool-Aid," Miss Anna said, "unless you would rather have milk this early in the morning."

I realized I had not eaten anything yet. "A glass of milk would be great," I said. I knew she would bring out cookies. For a woman who was so small and petite, Miss Anna loved her cookies.

When she finally sat down, she asked what was going on.

"I'm not really sure," I said. "I just needed to get away for a while."

Miss Anna gave me a sly look, as if to say she knew I was hiding something. But being the kind and considerate person that she was, she just smiled and pushed a container of cookies my way after taking one for herself.

"How are your parents?" Miss Anna asked. I don't think she suspected any problems; it was just something to break the silence.

"Actually," I started, "They are both having some issues lately."

Miss Anna just took another bite of her cookie.

"Dad is not feeling well," I said. "He's been looking pale and tired the past few days. He's not sleeping, and I'm getting worried about him."

"Blake takes a lot of medications as I recall," Miss Anna said. "Has he been to see Doctor Kane?"

"He hates going to the doctor, and he hates taking so many pills."

"I see."

"But Mom makes sure he takes his pills. In fact, she was just hounding him about taking his pills this morning."

"That's important."

"Mom has just been in a completely bad mood lately," I added. "It seems like we can't please her these days, no matter what we do."

"She works hard," Miss Anna said. "I see her leave in the morning and she doesn't get home until late at night."

I think she felt like she had been spying on us.

"It's hard to miss the headlights late at night," she added. "They sweep right across my living room windows when she turns into your driveway. Nobody else ever comes back here…"

I knew what she meant. Tangled Trail was a lonely place.

"Mom has been threatening to make Lizzy stay outside," I said. "I know Lizzy… she wouldn't make it long if she had to live outside."

"Why would your mom demand such a thing?"

I thought for just a second or two before answering. "There have been a couple of… mishaps lately," I said. "Mom just blamed Lizzy, even though I know Lizzy didn't do it."

"How do you know that?"

I stayed quiet for a moment. I had never lied to Miss Anna—other than those polite little white lies that prevent hurt feelings—and I didn't think she had ever lied to me. But something made it very difficult for me to say what I knew. I tried to think of something clever, but finally, I just said it. "Because the ghost did it."

Miss Anna adjusted herself in her chair. She brushed some loose hairs from her face and looked away for a moment. She turned back to me in seconds with a strange smirk on her face.

"You don't really believe that."

"Actually, I do," I said. "I wouldn't believe it if I had not seen it with my own eyes—and I wish I had not seen it—but I have."

A moment of uncomfortable silence passed between us. Miss Anna nervously nibbled at her ginger snap.

"I think the ghost is affecting my parents," I said. "My dad's illnesses have gotten worse since the ghost showed up. He's not sleeping, and he looks terrible. He's weak all the time, and it all started when the ghost became active."

Miss Anna was listening intently, eyes focused on me.

"My mom has grown distant. She and Dad don't sleep in the same room anymore. She stays at work later than ever and is always in a bad mood." I paused, reflecting on how things used to be. "She was never like that before."

I felt a little better having revealed my thoughts. I felt like I had uncovered some dark secret that was now there for someone else to see and help me think through.

"How many times have you seen the ghost?"

"It's not like the ghosts in the movies," I said. "Sometimes it's just shadows. Other times, it's a cool breeze blowing past." I took another bite of my cookie. "It can move things," I said. "It cries and moans and makes awful sounds…"

"How long has this been going on?"

"Just a few days," I said.

Miss Anna put her hands into a praying position, with the tips of her index fingers touching her upper lip.

"This is disturbing," she said.

I didn't expect that from her. She said she didn't believe in ghosts.

"What do you mean?" I asked. "Do you know something about the ghost?"

Miss Anna got the saddest, sweetest, most sympathetic look on her face. She reached out and took my hand in both of hers.

"Have you told your parents about the ghost?"

"No. I just don't know how to tell them, and they wouldn't believe me."

"You say the ghost looks like a shadow, and can move things?"

"Yes. It moves things around, like my dad's pills…"

Miss Anna squeezed my hands as she cut me off.

"Don't you realize what this means?" she asked. "Don't you understand?"

"No, I don't understand, and I want to. Who is this ghost? What do you know?"

Miss Anna paused and looked deeply into my eyes.

"I think I know who the ghost is," she said. "I think you know, too."

I was confused. It seemed like she was avoiding something, and that she didn't want to reveal what she knew. I had no idea who the ghost could be.

"Please tell me," I asked. "I think the ghost is affecting my mom and dad, and maybe me as well. I need to know what to do."

"It's you, Hadlee. It's you, my dear."

"Me?" It was an incredulous idea. "But I'm right here," I said. "I'm not a ghost, I'm still alive."

Miss Anna slowly shook her head, as if to say I didn't understand.

"Obviously you are not a ghost," she said. "But seeing shadows, finding things in places other than where you left them… that sounds to me like your mind playing tricks on you. You are simply seeing things that we all see and attributing it to a ghost. That's all, honey." She held her hands palms-up, as if offering me the solution on a platter.

"But the shadows, they moved like some kind of creepy spook," I said. "They are not like regular shadows, and the cold breeze that blows by when the ghost is near…"

"There are no such things as ghosts," Miss Anna said. "It's just your imagination."

"But Lizzy can see the ghost," I said. "She stares when there is nothing in the room and acts all weird when the ghost is near."

"Hadlee," Miss Anna said in a calming tone. "Are you still taking your anxiety meds?"

I shook my head. "They make me feel really strange sometimes," I said. "The co-pay is really expensive, too. My parents and I discussed it, and we all agreed that…"

Miss Anna interrupted me.

"Don't you see?" she said. "You are off your meds and your anxiety level has risen. You see shadows and think ghosts. Ghosts are on your mind. You misplace something and blame the ghost. Cool breezes? In that drafty old house of yours? Of course, you feel a draft sometimes."

"But what about…"

"Your cat? Cats are strange by nature. Cats will stare off into space just because they are cats. They're jumpy and skittish. I've had a few in my time. Never trust a cat."

"I hear strange noises, like moaning or crying."

"So do I, Sweetie, all the time. These old houses moan and groan when the wind hits them broadside, or even when the sun heats the siding. My house makes a lot of noise, and it's not because it's haunted."

"I know what I've seen," I said.

"Of course," Miss Anna replied. "I know you believe that you saw a ghost, but that doesn't mean you were right."

I sat quietly for a moment. I had been off my meds for a while, and I actually felt better than when I was on them. But I could not deny what she was saying. We both knew that my mind manifested things that were not real sometimes. But this was different. I was sure of it.

"I think your anxiety condition is worsening without your meds."

I could not argue.

I knew what I thought I had seen was real, but then again, I could stand in front of a group of elderly nuns and believe they were all hiding knives behind their backs, ready to stab me to death because I was such an unworthy person.

I got her point. Not everything I believed to be true actually was, and yet I could absolutely believe what I was feeling. That's part of my affliction. That's the symptoms I live with every day.

Miss Anna must have seen the fear on my face. She reached for my hands again and held them tightly.

"It's okay, Sweetheart," she said. "You will be fine. You should be back on your meds. If it's a matter of money, I'll pay for them. We can talk to your parents. I'm sure…"

Tears began to flow from my eyes, followed by loud sobs.

I felt so helpless.

Miss Anna stood, then pulled me to my feet. She wrapped her arms around me, her embrace soft and comforting. She was crying too.

"You will be okay, my dear. I'm sure you will be fine."

I leaned against her, still crying. I felt childish.

We finished crying, and I will say that I had never felt closer to Miss Anna than I did on that day. Emotionally, she was my grandmother—that trusted soul who was somehow beyond the scope of a parent.

I felt as if a tremendous hardship had been removed from me. It was certain in my mind that things would get back to normal after all, and this episode was simply an unfortunate series of events. While what Miss Anna said made sense to me, I was still not completely convinced that ghosts were not real.

Miss Anna and I sat quietly for a short time before I headed home, just enjoying our time together. Even though things were not as they seemed at the time, I still cherish being with her in that way, on that day.

Chapter 14

The garage door was open, and Mom's car was gone when I went back to the house. I looked in the garage to see if Lizzy might be hiding out there, but it was empty.

I checked on Dad first. I found him in his den, lying on the couch. He looked up at me with sad, painful eyes that were red where they should have been white. He was still pale but had taken on a grayish color. He had a robe on over some t-shirt and sweatpants.

I sat on his desk chair and rolled it toward him.

"You look awful," I said.

"You look beautiful, as usual."

He always said that, but I was his daughter and only child.

"Are you going to be okay? Can I get you something?"

"I'll be alright," he said weakly. "I think I picked up the flu somewhere."

"You should go to the doctor. You look that bad."

"Thanks." A slight smile played on his lips. "I'll give it a couple of days, and if I'm not better, I'll go."

The TV was on the Syfy channel—one of his favorites—but he wasn't watching it.

"Is everything okay with you and Mom?"

A hurt look played over his features.

"Not the best," he admitted.

It seemed he did not want to talk about it, but I was concerned and pressed on.

"What's going on?"

Dad shrugged. "Your mom is pretty stressed out," he said. "She feels like she has to work too much to make up for me…" He paused a moment. "Not working," he finally said. "Not having a real job."

I nodded. It was one of Mom's most frequent gripes.

"But I think I'm on to something good," Dad said. "I've been making some money lately, enough to make a difference."

I gave him a thumbs-up.

"She's also concerned about you," Dad went on.

"I know," I said.

"She doesn't want to push you, but also don't want to see you as a shut-in for your whole life."

An uncomfortable silence ensued for a moment.

"So, yeah, Mom's got a load of stress right now. I'm sure she will be fine, if we just give her some time and some space."

I gave Dad a hug. "You sure you don't need anything?"

"Some sleep," he replied. "I have not slept well in a few nights. I think that's part of my problem…"

He yawned and stretched his arms above his head.

"I'll let you try to sleep," I said. "I've got some things to do."

I left him with his TV on low volume and went to my room. There was an email in my inbox from Mary O'Reilly.

> *Dear Hadlee,*
> *You are right that animals often have the ability to sense ghosts. While your cat's behavior does not insure you have a ghost, just remember that pets often act strangely in the presence of a ghost.*
> *Most ghosts are simply lost souls trying to find their way in the afterlife. It's very rare that a ghost would pose any threat to the living.*

> *Understanding ghosts is the first step toward easing your fear. Just be aware that sometimes, a particular event, or changes in the ghost's environment might cause a normally docile spirit to become active in some way.*
> *So try not to be afraid, but if anything changes, please email or call me. I'm always willing to help an earthbound ghost move on.*
>
> *Mary*

I read the email twice. Mary included her phone number, which was nice of her.

While Miss Anna helped convince me there really was no ghost, I marked the email so that I could find it easily if something changed. But for the time being, I was happy just thinking that my mind had been playing tricks on me, and that all would return to normal on Tangled Trail.

But life has a way of changing circumstances, and life had a few surprises yet to throw my way.

Chapter 15

The day was unseasonably warm, and the sun felt wonderful on my face.

Lizzy was still not in the garage, and I was worried about her. The only other building on the property was a chicken coop that had been converted to a garden shed at the back of our yard. I had not been in there since the last warm days of fall and hoped I would find Lizzy there.

The red barn paint had all but worn off the shed, leaving the gray, weathered wood exposed to the sunlight. The small windows were so dirty there was no way to see inside. There was a small door on one end that allowed chickens access back in the day. The shed was one of Lizzy's favorite haunts.

The door for people was on the far end of the shed, and I swung it open wide to let more light in. The door squealed on rusted hinges, coming to rest against the side of the building. Dust motes hung in the air, and the room smelled of aged wood and old straw.

Movement caught my eye. I found Lizzy lying on an old burlap bag. She stood upon seeing me, arching her back and then stretching her legs in a feline yoga pose. She looked at me and gave a weak meow. She seemed calm and rested. I reached down and stroked her back. She arched higher with each stroke, purring and content.

Various garden tools hung on the walls, relics of years gone by. Neither of my parents did any gardening. These tools had been here since I can remember. I'm sure they had belonged to the DuVall family ages ago.

Most were rusted and covered in cobwebs and dust, but some still had the faint gleam of polished metal, ornate in the way of things made long ago. An old wooden crate sat in one corner. I dusted it off and sat on it, hoisting Lizzy onto my lap.

It was peaceful in the shed. Quiet. The dust motes danced on the breeze coming in the door, and Lizzy was warm and soft. I was content to sit there, studying the old tools and other items that had sat in the same spots since well before I was born—perhaps since before my parents were born. Miss Anna would know about them, likely having watched a hired hand use them in her youth. She often told stories of how her family had hired help. She said that she was closer to the servants than she was to her own family, and it was a maid named Lilly who actually raised her. Miss Anna's mother had been frail and died young, and it was Lilly who tended to little Anna and Emma for most of their childhood.

While lost in my thoughts, I wasn't sure if I sat there for mere moments, or for an hour, but my peaceful time came to a sudden end when the door slammed shut violently, casting the room in near darkness.

Before I could comprehend what had happened, Lizzy leaped and disappeared in the dark corners of the shed.

The air had been stirred by the slamming of the door, filling the shed with floating dust. The weak light from the windows made it look like the room was filled with a light, smoky haze. Just as suddenly, the door flung itself open, banging loudly against the outside wall. The room was bright again, dust falling in rivulets from the rafters, swirling in the patterns of the air currents.

I held my breath—partially from fear—as the dust filled my nostrils. The tools began to rattle against the walls; the sounds of metal against hard wood filled my head.

Once again, the door slammed shut, then back open.

The sunlight outside beckoned me, and I finally found the will to move. I ran through the door, craving the fresh air.

The shed door crashed shut behind me, but I didn't look back. The back porch of the house was in sight, and I focused on that. Everything was a blur, but my mind was screaming that I was not hallucinating. This was real. Meds or no meds, this was happening.

I stumbled through the house, banging my thigh against the kitchen counter as I turned down the hall to my dad's den. I wanted to be near him. I knew he could calm me down.

I galloped down the hallway and burst into his room, panting.

Dad was lying on the couch, just where I left him earlier. His eyes were squeezed shut, a look of pain on his face.

I screamed at him, and reached for his hand, which dangled near the floor. His skin was cool and clammy. Beads of sweat dotted his grayish-colored face.

I dropped to my knees, holding his hand in mine, screaming.

Then his body began to bounce, as if some invisible hands were pushing down on him, then releasing him, then pushing down again. He flopped around on the couch like a landed fish. He would not respond to me, just held this pained look on his face.

In my tortured mind, I knew the ghost was killing my dad. It pounded him violently, causing him to jerk and shudder.

"Stop!" I screamed. "Leave him alone!"

I laid myself across him, feeling the jolts through my core.

Then he laid still, gasping for breath.

Tears filled my eyes as I looked at him. I was in shock, and scared into a mindless frenzy. After a moment, I realized I needed to call 9-1-1. We had a land-line attached to a fax machine that Mom used for work. I dashed down the hall, picked up the receiver, willing my fingers to work.

I heard a voice answer, hardly understanding anything she said. I confirmed the address, unable to get the words out in any reasonable order. I don't exactly recall what I said, but the dispatcher assured me an ambulance was on its way.

I ran back to my dad, who was still breathing, his eyes open to moist slits. His arms moved as he pulled them slowly to his chest. I talked to him; the urgency for him to respond was evident in my weak voice.

"An ambulance is coming," I said. "Hang in there, Dad. Please hang in there."

Dad groaned.

I heard gravel crunching in the driveway, surprised that the ambulance had arrived so quickly. I realized it wasn't the ambulance when Mom's car drove past, heading to the garage. I ran to the back door to meet her, certain she would know what to do to help Dad.

I got to the back door as Mom came up the steps. I grabbed the doorknob to pull it open but met an unusual resistance. I pulled again, but the door only moved an inch, then slammed shut.

It was happening again.

Mom must have seen the panic on my face. She pushed from her side, but the door would not budge.

"It's stuck!" I shouted. I fumbled with the lock to no avail. "Dad is sick," I called through the glass.

"I'll go to the front door," Mom called back.

She dropped her bags and disappeared around the corner of the house. The front door was always locked and seldom used. I ran through the house and turned the ancient deadbolt. It was always a tricky thing to unlock that door, but the mechanism released. I pulled on the door, but it remained in place.

Mom got there and looked at me through the window with a mixture of fear and annoyance. She pulled the screen door open and put her shoulder against the heavy wooden door. She pushed, and I could see the door give way, then pull itself closed again. After several tries, Mom looked at me dumbfounded.

"What are you doing?" she yelled through the glass.
"Nothing!" I'm not touching it!"

I grabbed the handle and pulled as Mom pushed. I could feel the door move slightly—it definitely was not latched—but some force was keeping it from opening.

Mom and I argued through the glass as I made sure the lock was not engaged.

Mom started to back away from the door. "I'm going to the back door again," she said. She turned to go down the steps and was suddenly falling. It looked to me as if she were pushed. Her arms pinwheeled as she tried to get her balance, but she stumbled and ended up face down in the grass.

I screamed again, pulling on the door frantically to get it open.
"Leave us alone!" I screamed.
I heard sirens on the highway.

Mom rolled around in the grass and finally sat up, clutching her left wrist in her right hand.

The trees had not yet leafed out, and I saw the flashing lights of the ambulance as it traced a path through the woods.

Mom got up, looking a bit weak, and turned to the ambulance. A fire truck was close behind it. They both stopped in a cloud of dust and people poured out the doors.

"The door is stuck," I heard Mom say to the firemen.

I took the knob in my hand as the first fireman approached and pulled. The door opened smoothly. I was simultaneously startled and relieved.

As the paramedics and fire personnel approached the house, my symptoms kicked in. I got short of breath, and my face felt flushed. My hands began to shake. I stepped back into the hall and pointed the way to Dad's den, unable to speak.

Mom followed them in, still clutching her wrist.

I was angry with myself. My dad was sick, and I was like a scared little mouse, cowering to avoid the people there to help. I felt ashamed.

Once the hallway cleared, I could hear people talking from Dad's room. One of the paramedics was shouting his name.

"Blake, can you hear me? Blake! Blake! Talk to me, Blake." More muted conversation and I heard someone say *He's convulsing*.

Two more people with the ambulance came with a gurney. They parked it on the front porch and loosened the straps.

One of them looked at me. He had a kind face, and a big, bushy moustache. "Are you okay?"

I nodded as I melted further back in the hallway.

A deputy sheriff parked closer to Miss Anna's house. He walked up to the porch and greeted the guys with the gurney. He stepped past them and into the front room.

I pointed down the hall. The deputy nodded and pulled out a pad of paper.

"What's your name?" he asked.

I told him as he jotted.

"Are you the one who called 9-1-1?"

I nodded again.

"Is it your dad who is sick? What's his name?"

There was more jotting on the pad and more questions. How old is he? Where does he work? How long has he lived here? What's his date of birth? Is he married? What's his wife's name?

The endless questions caused me to panic. I started breathing hard. The next thing I know, Miss Anna was standing in the doorway.

She brushed past the deputy and put her arms around me, standing between me and the deputy. "That's enough for now," she told the deputy.

"Take a deep breath," she said to me. "What's going on?"

"Dad is sick," I answered.

She guided me outside and into the yard. She wiped my tears away with a tissue she had in her pocket.

"Stay calm, my dear," she said. "Everything will be okay."

I knew she meant well, and I loved her for her caring touch, but I also knew there was no way for her to know everything would be okay. It's just the standard line you tell someone who is going through something bad. It's another white lie.

Miss Anna managed to calm me down. My breathing evened out. I had just stopped crying when the ambulance crew wheeled the gurney onto the porch with my dad strapped to it. Seeing my dad on that gurney caused the tears to flow again.

Dad was a big guy, and it took several firemen to lift the gurney carefully down the porch steps and onto the ground. Dad was covered with white linens and had an oxygen mask on his face. I couldn't tell if his eyes were open or not. One fireman carried an IV bag with a line that went somewhere under the linens.

Miss Anna held me close, saying soothing things and kissing my wet cheeks.

Mom followed the paramedics out. She had dirt and grass stains on the knee of her light-green slacks. She held her left hand across her abdomen, her fingers dangling.

She looked at me and Miss Anna.

"They want me to ride with the ambulance," she said. She looked right to Miss Anna. "You'll watch over Hadlee?"

Both of them knew I could not tolerate going to the hospital. That would have been like hell on earth for me.

"Of course," Miss Anna replied. "We'll be fine. You have my number, so keep us informed."

Mom climbed into the ambulance. A few minutes later, it pulled away. Within a few minutes, the firetruck left as well.

The deputy stepped into the front yard. He looked at Miss Anna as if to ask if it was okay to approach.

"How old are you, Hadlee?"

He had his paper and pen out.

"Seventeen," I answered. "My birthday is in two more days," I added.

Endless jotting.

He looked at Miss Anna.

"What's your name, ma'am?"

"Anna DuVall," she said. "I live next door."

"Hadlee will be staying with you until her mom gets back?"

Miss Anna just nodded.

The deputy walked toward his car, talking into his portable radio.

Miss Anna placed a hand on each of my shoulders and looked into my weepy eyes. "Will you be more comfortable here, or at my house?"

"Your house," I said without hesitation. I didn't want to go back into my house. There was a ghost in my house, but I didn't say that.

Chapter 16

I didn't want to talk. Miss Anna seemed to understand, giving me space and not asking many questions. I sat in her living room while she puttered around in her kitchen. She checked in on me every few minutes, sometimes just giving me a look, sometimes asking if I needed anything.

For the first time, I looked closely at the family pictures hanging on her walls. They were all old. There were no color pictures at all. It was as if her family ceased to exist in the days of black and white. Miss Anna was the only one who made it to the age of color, but there were no pictures of her. I guess there was nobody around to take a photo of her.

My family did take photos. We didn't hang them on the walls, but they were on my dad's computer. They were mostly of him and me together, when Mom snapped a photo on her cell phone. Many were from my birthday or at Christmas, just me and Mom and Dad. We didn't go places like normal families because of my condition. But there were pictures, and looking at them now is like revisiting the moments when my family smiled.

Unlike most teenagers, I didn't have a cell phone. I rarely left the house, and when I did, I was with Mom or Dad. We had the land-line, so a cell phone for me would have been a waste.

As I sat in Miss Anna's living room, the sound of a car and the reflected sunlight alerted me to a visitor. I looked out the window and saw two police cars pull up in front of my house. Miss Anna must have heard it too.

All I could think was that the police were returning to deliver bad news. I began crying again; just knowing they would tell me my dad was dead. I wanted to shrink into a tiny ball and become lost, so nobody could find me. I was not ready. There had not been time to prepare myself.

Two officers wearing different uniforms got out of the cars. There was a woman with them. She was slender and walked with an air of confidence. I could see hints of red in her brown hair as she followed the officers to Miss Anna's front door.

The knock was anything but gentle. Police do not knock on doors gently. Miss Anna opened the door.

"Miss Duvall?" the first officer asked. He was tall and lanky, with a bit of a belly. He had gray hair curling under his hat. The other officer was tall and athletic. He stood close to the woman. "I'm Sheriff Norm Oberlin, and this is Chief Bradley Alden." He pointed to the other cop. "We need to speak with Hadlee," he said.

"Come in," Miss Anna said.

I knew what was coming and I sobbed out loud. I felt that I would become part of the chair, unable to stand or move. I had watched scenes like this on TV.

Miss Anna came to my side, placing a hand on my shoulder.

The woman stepped into the room. She gave me a sympathetic smile that whispered *friend*, as she approached me. She dropped to one knee and took my hand.

"Hadlee, I'm Mary," she said. "Mary O'Reilly."

The name was familiar, but out of context. I knew the name, but my mind raced to place it. A few seconds later, it dawned on me.

"What are you doing here?" I blurted. "How could you…"

"Can we talk?" Mary asked.

"Is my dad dead?"

Mary looked surprised. "Not that I'm aware of." She glanced at the Sheriff.

"Your dad is in intensive care at Freeport Memorial," Sheriff Oberlin offered. "He's not dead, but he's in bad shape. They're taking good care of him."

"Can we talk?" Mary repeated.

I nodded.

"We need to talk outside," Chief Alden said.

Mary gave me a warm, compassionate look. "Can we do that?" she asked. "Can we step outside?"

I reached out and she took my hands, gently pulling me out of the chair. She wrapped an arm around me and pulled me close as we made our way to the door. Chief Alden followed, and the Sheriff stayed with Miss Anna.

Miss Anna had a bench along the sidewalk in her front yard. Mary led me there and we both sat.

"You know why I'm here, right?" she asked.

"You talk to ghosts," I said. "But how did you know... Why are you with the police?"

"This is my husband, Bradley," she said, waving a hand at Chief Alden.

"Just call me Bradley," he said.

"You called 9-1-1 earlier, right?" Mary asked.

I bobbed my head.

"You told the dispatcher that a ghost was trying to kill your father."

"I did?" I was honestly surprised. I didn't remember saying that, but it had been like a blur to me.

"Well... I'm the ghost lady," Mary said. "The dispatcher got in touch with Bradley, and here I am."

There was that smile again. "Tell me what happened."

It was as if the words came out in a flood. I told Mary about the ghost, what I had seen and felt over the past few days. She listened intently, and I could tell she believed what I was saying. It felt so good to have an adult believe this crazy story that I hardly believed myself. I left out no detail. I told her about the dolls, the sounds, the doors slamming, and the papers being scattered around the room. I told her how the pills had come flying out of the cupboard, and how Lizzy was afraid of the ghost.

I kept glancing up at Bradley. He didn't flinch. I guessed he had heard stories like mine before.

"Can you see the ghost?" I asked.

"Not yet," Mary replied. "Sometimes they can be a little shy." She glanced over at my house. "Is it okay if I go over and sit on your porch?"

"Sure," I said.

Mary stood up. "Why don't you go back inside," she said. "I might be a little while."

I headed back inside, while Mary and Bradley walked toward my house.

When I got to Miss Anna's porch, she was waiting for me.

"Your mother is on the phone," she said.

Miss Anna's phone was in the kitchen. She stayed in the living room with the Sheriff.

"Hello?"

"I'm still at the hospital," Mom said. "They are still trying to find out what's wrong with your dad."

"Is he awake?"

"No, honey, he is still unconscious. They are running all kinds of tests."

Neither of us spoke for a few seconds.

"Are you okay, Hadlee?"

"No," I said. I was on the verge of tears and Mom could hear it in my voice.

"Stay strong," she said. "We'll get through this."

"How are you doing?" I asked.

"Okay, considering," she said.

"Considering what?"

"Well, considering that I broke a bone in my arm when I fell off the porch."

"Really?"

"Yes, really. They have my arm splinted right now. They'll put a cast on it shortly."

"Wow. I'm sorry, Mom."

There was another brief silence.

"You stay with Anna, and I'll be home when I can," she said.

The call ended.

I went back to the living room. The Sheriff had gone outside. Miss Anna was peeking out the window to my house.

"What are they doing over there?" she asked.

"I'm not sure." *Another white lie.* I just didn't want to go there again with Miss Anna.

"It looks like they are just standing on the porch, talking."

I didn't say anything.

She turned to me. "What did your mother say?"

"Dad's still unconscious. The hospital is running tests."

She offered a sympathetic look.

"Oh, and Mom broke her arm," I said. I explained what happened, leaving out the part about the ghost.

A few minutes later, Mary and the officers returned. I stepped outside when I saw them crossing the yard.

Mary wasn't smiling anymore. The look on her face was serious. She must have seen something.

Bradley and the Sheriff stood by the police cars, talking. Mary continued my way, but her expression didn't change.

"Did you see a ghost?"

Mary didn't answer.

"We have some work to do," she said. "But I'll be back later, and I'll tell you everything."

"Tell me now," I said.

Mary got a sad look. "I can't, Sweetie," she said. "But I promise I will be back soon, and I will explain everything then."

"Then tell me if we have a ghost," I said. "So that I know if I'm even crazier than I thought."

Mary put a hand on each of my arms.

"You have a ghost," she said. "But trust me; it's not what you think."

She turned away and walked toward the police cars. "You get some rest," she said. "I'll be back."

She ducked into Bradley's car. Both vehicles drove down Tangled Trail, weaving through the trees.

Had I known then, what I know now, I would have taken Mary's advice and gotten some rest. I was in for the longest night of my life.

Chapter 17

I was on edge the rest of that afternoon. Mom didn't call again from the hospital, and Mary O'Reilly had not come back. I was anxious to find out what Mary meant with her cryptic message about the ghost, and that she would tell me everything later. Why later? What was she holding back from me?

But Mary seemed like someone I could trust—and for me that was a big deal. There were very few people I was comfortable being around. I was never comfortable in a crowd, but there had been a few people outside of Tangled Trail that I was comfortable with one-on-one. The nurse at my doctor's office, Janice, was one of them. Once I got past the lobby and into a room with Janice, I was fine. She was open, caring, and honest. She didn't seem threatening in the least.

Another was one of my mom's business associates, Rosie, but for different reasons. Rosie was confident but friendly. She could even be loud and boisterous, but in a benevolent, outgoing way. She liked to joke—but it was always good-natured. Rosie was fun to be around.

I got those same vibes from Mary O'Reilly. I liked her, even though I had met her under dire circumstances.

The tall trees surrounding the houses on Tangled Trail cast long shadows as sunset approached. I wondered if Mary meant that she would return that same night, or the next day. She hadn't really said.

The phone rang in the kitchen, and Miss Anna called to me.

"It's your mom."

Mom told me that there was no change in Dad's condition, but that he was stable for the time being. They were waiting for test results. She said she would be home soon, and to come home when I saw her pull in.

Miss Anna prepared some mac-n-cheese and made ham sandwiches. I hadn't realized how hungry I was until it was put in front of me.

Just as I finished, headlights swept past the windows. I looked out and saw two more police vehicles pull up. Mary got out the passenger side of Bradley's car. Sheriff Oberlin and a deputy got out of another car and leaned on the fenders.

I went to Mary to find out what was going on.

"Hi, Hadlee" she said. She gave me a hug. I got a lot of hugs that day, and there were more to come.

"How is your dad?" Mary asked.

"He's stable, but still unconscious. Mom called just a little while ago. She said she would be home soon."

"We're saying prayers for him, honey."

"Thanks." I moved some gravel around with the toe of my shoe. "What are you doing here?"

"Waiting for your Mom," she said. "The police have some questions for her."

Police always had lots of questions; it was their job.

"You said we have a ghost."

Mary hesitated. "You do, Sweetie. But like I said, you won't understand."

She clearly did not want to say more. I didn't push her, because I trusted her.

"Let's wait for your mom, and then things will be clear."

"Okay," I said.

"I've heard about your condition," Mary said. "I want you to know that you will be fine. You stay strong and know that Bradley and I care about you."

That didn't sound good. It sounded like a preparation for bad news. Bad news also makes me anxious, and tears began to flow.

Mary gave me another hug.

I saw headlights through the trees coming toward the house. I could tell by the familiar sound that it was Mom's car. She drove right past the police cars and into the garage, not bothering to close the garage door. The Sheriff stepped out to meet her.

"Joyce Monroe?"

Mom stopped a few feet away. "Yes?"

"Ma'am, we have a warrant to search the property."

Mom's jaw visibly dropped. "A warrant? For what?"

"It's a warrant to search these premises for evidence of a crime." The Sheriff handed Mom the paperwork.

"What are you talking about?" Mom said.

The moment she said it, I knew something was wrong. Mom was not being herself. The way she responded told me she knew something and was putting on a show. She didn't answer like the Joyce Monroe that I knew. She was being an actress.

By this time, Miss Anna had come out of her house, wrapping herself in a long sweater. She came directly to my side. She had heard what the Sheriff had said. She squeezed my arm.

Mom was pretending to look over the papers. They trembled in her hands.

"I refuse to cooperate," Mom said. "You will all leave now."

Her voice was weak, ready to break. Her bottom lip quivered.

"I'm afraid we can't do that, Ma'am," the Sheriff said. "We have a warrant to search the premises for evidence of a crime. You can be present during this search, or you can be taken in for further questioning, but these premises will be searched."

Mom stomped up the stairs on the front porch. "At least let me tidy up some things inside," she said.

The Sheriff climbed the stairs and took Mom by the arm.

"Can't do that, Missus Monroe," he said as he pulled her back. "You will be under observation during the search."

Mom pulled her arm away from the Sheriff.

"Mary?" The Sheriff said as he glanced her way.

Mary whispered into my ear. "I'm so sorry, Hadlee," then she walked up the stairs. The deputy and Bradley followed me and Miss Anna inside.

I was completely lost. My mind was not putting together things as they happened. I felt a strange sense of déjà vu, like this was part of some movie that I had already seen. It was as if my emotions were somehow detached from the circumstances.

Mary walked down the hall to Dad's den, then walked back. She walked through the empty front room, her steps slow and methodical.

The rest of us just stayed out of her way.

"What is this?" Mom asked. "I thought you were going to search."

The Sheriff just ignored her. The deputy kept an eye on her.

Mary walked into the kitchen. As she walked around the corner of the table, she pulled up short, as if to avoid something. She got a peculiar look on her face. She stared into space, as if looking at something nobody else could see.

The ghost.

Mary held up her hands, as if to ask for quiet. She nodded on occasion.

"Joyce has been poisoning Blake," Mary said.

I looked at Mom. Her face drained of color.

Mary directed Sheriff Oberlin to the cabinets above the refrigerator—the very cabinet the pills came flying out of earlier that morning. The Sheriff donned a pair of latex gloves and reached into the cabinet. He withdrew the same two bottles of pills and examined them.

"That's some of Blake's prescriptions," Mom said. "Look, they have his name on them."

The Sheriff looked at the bottles. Without a word, he dropped them into an evidence bag.

Mary was staring straight ahead again, then nodded an apparent affirmation.

"There are more pills," Mary said. "They're in Joyce's bedroom."

The entire entourage followed Mary to the back of the house. The deputy followed Mom.

"Bottom corner of the closet," Mary said. "There is a fireproof safe box. It's locked."

The Sheriff opened the closet door and swept back some clothes. He bent over and slid a heavy, gray safe box into the middle of the room. The Sheriff looked at Mom.

"Key, please."

"I don't know where it is," Mom said. "I have not had that thing opened in a long time."

The Sheriff looked at Mary.

"In her purse," Mary said. "It's in a zipped pouch in her wallet."

The deputy took hold of Mom's purse, but Mom pulled it back.

"You have no right to…"

The Sheriff spoke up. "The warrant gives us the explicit right to search anything on these premises."

Mom still struggled with the deputy.

"Missus Monroe," the Sheriff said. "I don't want to cuff you in front of your daughter, but make no mistake—I will if I need to."

Mom gave up and handed the deputy her purse.

He found the key exactly where Mary said it would be.

The Sheriff opened the safe and found another bottle of pills. They were small, red pills. I had seen Dad take them.

"You will find that those pills are deadly when combined with Blake's other prescriptions," Mary said.

Sheriff Oberlin took the pill bottle in his gloved hand and deposited it into another evidence bag.

I was numb, still in a weird state of emotionless observation—like the scientific method. I was like a stand-in for Hadlee Monroe.

Miss Anna shadowed my every step, staying close and keeping in physical contact with me. I could hear her gasp when Mary revealed something.

Mary raised her hands and looked at the Sheriff. "There's nothing more," she said.

"We will be confiscating all computers and cell phones," the Sheriff said to Mom. "We need to do a routine search of the premises." He looked at Mom. "Missus Monroe, I need you in the squad car. Please cooperate."

Mom said nothing. The deputy led her away.

Sheriff Oberlin directed his attention to Miss Anna and me. "I need you two to leave the house now," he said. "Mary, would you please?"

Mary nodded and walked with us to the front door. When I saw Mom in the back of the squad car, I lost it. That peaceful, detached feeling went away, and the world came crushing down on me. My legs turned to rubber. My balance was off, and I teetered like a drunk. Miss Anna had me by one arm and Mary had the other. They led me to Miss Anna's house. I asked to sit on a chair on the front porch, out of sight of the deputy's squad car. The air was cool and there was a light breeze.

I realized that my sheltered world was changing. Nothing would ever be the same. There was no fixing this—regardless of Dad's outcome—the deed was done and could never be reversed. My parents were finished, one way or another.

Tangled Trail

Miss Anna and Mary pulled up chairs close to mine. I could feel the love and pity from them both. I could feel their hearts breaking for me.

We sat on that front porch for a long time while the officers carted things out of the house. After what seemed hours, the deputy's vehicle drove away. It was too dark to see inside, but I knew my Mom was being taken to jail. I felt very much alone.

The lights were on at my house, shedding light into the yard between the houses. I noticed a pair of dark shapes coming across the yard. It was the Sheriff and Bradley.

They came up the steps and the Sheriff squatted down in front of me.

"Hadlee, I understand that you are seventeen years old. Is that correct?"

"Yes," I said. "My birthday is the day after tomorrow."

"I know you've had a hard day, but we need to figure out what to do with you. I can't leave you alone."

"She can stay right here," Miss Anna said. "I have plenty of room."

"That's kind of you, ma'am," he said. "But we need to place her with family if at all possible."

"I don't have any family," I said. "Not around here, anyway."

Sheriff Oberlin nodded. "We can make short-term arrangements for now," he said. "In two days, you will be of legal age and can make your own decisions. So, for now, if you would like to stay with Miss DuVall, we can make that happen."

Miss Anna patted my shoulder.

"Your house is still an active crime scene," the Sheriff said. "We can accompany you inside to get your personal items, but after that, you cannot go inside without an officer present."

Mary stood. "Let's go get you some clothes."

Miss Anna took my hand and we followed the others to my house. Bradley lifted the yellow tape declaring my house a crime scene. Miss Anna and I ducked under.

Mary and Miss Anna came with me to my room. I didn't have any luggage, so we packed some clothes into shopping bags.

When I finished packing, I noticed Miss Anna looking at the doll house, fiddling with some of the furniture. When she turned to me, her eyes were red and moist.

"Silly me," she said. "With all that has gone on today, it's this doll house that makes me emotional."

Mary gave Miss Anna a gentle hug. "It been a hard day for everyone," she said. "Emotions are running high."

I left my room on Tangled Trail, not knowing if I would never return. I turned out the light and followed the others down the hall.

We got to the kitchen where the Sheriff and Bradley awaited us. The Sheriff glanced at my shopping bags, then to Mary who nodded to signal we had what we needed.

The lights in the kitchen began to flicker.

Mary took my arm and held it tight. "The ghost is back," she said.

I don't know what Miss Anna thought of all of this. We had not had a chance to talk about it. It would be hard to deny that Mary was getting information from somewhere, and a ghost fit the evidence.

"The ghost has more to say," Mary said. "She says it's time for the truth."

Miss Anna nearly fell. Bradley helped her into a kitchen chair.

"She died a long time ago," Mary went on. "There was a love triangle, and things got out of hand."

The Sheriff looked at me, and then back to Mary.

"It was an accidental death that was covered up," Mary went on, "loved ones who were fighting."

Mary fell silent, cocking her head as if tracking something. She turned to Miss Anna.

"It was your sister," Mary said. "Her name is Anna."

"Her sister's name was Emma," I said, as if the entire world should know this. "This is Anna." I pointed to my neighbor.

Both the Sheriff and Bradley were staring at Miss Anna.

"No," Mary said. "Anna is on the other side. Anna is the one who is talking to me." She turned to Miss Anna. "You're Emma," Mary said flatly.

"Hogwash," Miss Anna said. "My sister Emma ran away when she was young, never to be heard from again. It was a long time ago, and that's all in the past. Please don't make me relive the pain of losing her again with your silly stories."

Mary looked to Bradley and the Sheriff. "This is what I'm getting," she said. "I'm speaking to Anna DuVall, and she claims to have died in this house."

"This is rubbish," Miss Anna shouted. "You claim to speak with ghosts, but who says the ghost is telling the truth?" Miss Anna straightened up in her chair. "Emma is gone, presumed dead for some sixty years now."

Mary focused again. "Anna says that she loves you, Emma, and that she is sorry for what happened. She doesn't blame you, but she needs to move on."

The woman I knew as Miss Anna sobbed. I was so confused.

"Her body is in a cistern, under the house," Mary said. "She wants this secret revealed so that she can move on to the light."

Miss Anna's hand was over her mouth and tears flowed freely. She stood and walked to the back door.

"I'm going home," she said. She opened the door and walked out into the dark.

Mary looked at Bradley and the Sheriff.

"We can't do anything," the Sheriff said. "We need proof. If you say there is a body, we need to recover it, and that's not going to happen tonight."

"She's not going anywhere," Bradley said. "We have time to sort this out."

"What about me?" I asked.

The adults all looked at each other.

"Under the circumstances, I think we have to find another place for you. I don't think Miss DuVall is up for company right now."

Mary and Bradley nodded in agreement.

"I'd like to see my dad," I said. I did not want to go to the hospital, but I did want to see my dad. He wasn't going anywhere, so I had to go to him.

"It's late, and there will not be many people there," I added. "Can that be worked out?"

The Sheriff was nodding his head. "I think we can work that out, if we escort you."

Bradley and Mary volunteered to take me. Mary had an idea about where I could stay and said she would make some phone calls.

I had other questions for the ghost. That ghost owed me some answers, and I felt I should have them.

Chapter 18

It was almost midnight when we left Tangled Trail and drove toward Freeport, some twenty minutes away.

Bradley was the Chief of Police in Freeport, so he could get me into the hospital with no problems. I was on the verge of a breakdown of some kind, with all my potential ailments and issues. But I tried to maintain that disconnected attitude. Life was always a challenge and was always going to be. I had to suck it up and get through this horrific time in my life. For my dad, I was willing to take the chance.

Mary was in the front seat, and I asked her a question.

"How do you know the ghost is not lying?"

Mary glanced over her shoulder. "Ghosts have very little reason to lie," she said. "I can also get a feel for a ghost. I can tell if they seem agitated, angry, or evil in some way. Anna's ghost strikes me as desperate to move on."

"I can't think of Miss Anna as Emma," I blurted. "I've known her as Anna for my whole life."

"Stranger things have happened," Mary said. "At this point, I take the ghost at its word. It really has no reason to lie."

"But Miss Anna... I mean Emma... is such a kind and gentle person. She is like a grandmother to me. I just can't believe something like this happened."

A police report came over the radio, and Bradley had to answer. When he finished, I asked him a question.

"What's going to happen to Miss Anna?"

"We will see if there is a body under the house," he said. We have to get another warrant to do that, and then we will send a crew to investigate."

"Will she have to go to prison?"

"Doubtful," Bradley replied. "A judge will decide that. There has to be an investigation, then likely a hearing, and it goes on from there. It all depends on what we find."

Bradley parked his cruiser near the Emergency Room entrance.

He escorted me and Mary to my father's room. We encountered only a handful of people along the way.

I was shocked when I walked into the darkened room and saw my dad. There were all kinds of tubes and wires attached to him, and all kinds of blinking and beeping machines monitoring him. He had a tube down his throat, with tape across his face to keep it in place.

I tried to hold up. I tried to keep that disconnect working for me, but I failed. I could not see my dad like that and not break down.

Mary stood beside me, a hand on my shoulder.

I was afraid to touch my dad. There were so many fragile and delicate things hooked to him that I feared I would break or disconnect something. Even his index finger had a glowing device attached to it. I placed my hand on his shoulder. I could feel him hanging on, life still flowing through him.

"Be strong, Dad," I sobbed. "Just like you always tell me to do. I need you here."

I hoped he could hear me. I hoped that he was having a dream of his daughter standing beside him, encouraging him to hang on. I hoped he could hear the love in my voice.

I realized that this could be the last time I would ever see him, and even though I held out hope for a full recovery, I wanted him to hear something that could be my last words to him.

"I love you, Dad."

I kissed his forehead, then backed away from him. Bradley took my arm and gently led me into the hallway.

Mary was outside the door, looking at something on her phone. She put it away and joined me and Bradley.

"You can stay with us tonight," she said. "It's far too late to find another place, but I have an idea for a great place where you can stay until you can get on your feet."

"Thank you," I said. "You are both so kind."

We left the hospital. The roads had almost no traffic at this time of night. Then a thought hit me.

"Oh my God, Lizzy!"

Bradley hit the brakes, thinking something was terribly wrong.

"Who's Lizzy?" Mary asked, looking over the back of the seat.

"I'm sorry," I said. "Lizzy is my cat."

Bradley sped up again.

"Poor Lizzy seems to have been tormented by the ghost," I said. "It seems each time her and I were together, the ghost came, and Lizzy would run. She finally got outside, and I didn't think to leave any food for her. I know she has not eaten in a few days. She is not normally outside at night... she must be scared to death."

"We can't have that," Mary said. She turned to Bradley. "It's not that far. Can't we stop?"

Bradley nodded. "Sure," he said. "This won't be my first cat rescue, and likely not my last."

"I don't think he really wanted to go back to my house, but he was too polite to say so. Maybe he just wasn't a cat person.

With no traffic it didn't take long at all to get to Willow River. We pulled up in front of my house, and I swear I have never seen the house so dark.

"The cat food is inside," I said. "Lizzy usually comes running if I shake the bag."

I suggested we go in the back door, and I called for Lizzy as we walked around the house. Bradley led us inside and found the kitchen light switch. I walked to the pantry and reached for the cat food.

As I turned, I saw Mary staring down the dark hallway.

"Anna is back," she said. She nodded, and as I watched a strange look came over Mary's face. She then started shaking her head from side to side, as if to deny something.

"Sit down, Hadlee," Mary instructed.

I prepared myself. I knew more bad news was coming my way. I didn't think I could tolerate it.

"My dad?" I said in a barely audible voice.

Mary was still staring down the hall, but she turned to me. "No, it's not about your dad," Mary said. Bradley stepped up behind my chair.

"I'm looking at Anna," Mary said. "Your neighbor—who is actually Emma..." She paused, as if searching for the right words. "Emma is with her."

It took me a few seconds to understand what she meant. I was confused again, but it finally sank in.

"No, God, please," I cried. "Why is this happening?"

I sank into my chair, burying my face in my hands. I looked up, and Mary was backing toward the table, still looking down the hall.

Mary turned to me. "They are both here," she said. "The one you know as Miss Anna, is truly Emma. She acknowledges that."

"But, why?" I asked, still sobbing.

"Emma is saying that it's complicated," said Mary. "But she fell in love with a man, and her twin sister, the real Anna, stole him away from her. Anna became engaged to the man. Emma was distraught and depressed, and thought of running away."

I started to say something, but Mary raised her hand.

"Anna is stepping forward now," she said. "She is confirming this. The two sisters had a fight. Anna was hitting Emma, and

Emma grabbed Anna to push her away. Anna stumbled, and fell out the open upstairs window."

I saw Mary swallow hard.

"Anna's neck was broken," Mary continued. "She was dead by the time Emma got to her. Emma panicked, and dragged Anna's body to the old cistern, that had recently been filled in when indoor plumbing was installed. She buried Anna there."

Mary took a deep breath.

"It was an accident!" I shouted. "Why not just tell the truth?"

Mary looked at me, then turned back to the ghosts.

"Because she was jealous, and wanted Anna's fiancée," Mary said. "She was young and foolish and scared. She wasn't thinking, just reacting." Mary was silent again. "Once the deed was done and the lies were told, there was no going back.

"Everyone knew that Emma had been depressed and threatening to run away, so Emma wrote a note and left it for her father to find, saying she was leaving. She then pretended to be Anna for the rest of her life."

"But how could that work?" I asked. "Couldn't her father tell them apart?"

Mary turned back to the hallway, where the two stood as apparitions that only Mary could see.

"Emma is talking again," Mary said. "She says her father was involved in many other things, always busy, never paying attention to details. Nobody knew Anna better than she did. She says she simply began acting like Anna would, and before long, she had become Anna.

"Anna's fiancée never said it, but he knew something was different. He left after their father began building the house that was to be Anna's wedding present, so her father had no choice but to finish the house.

"But Emma didn't fool everyone," Mary went on. "Lilly, the housekeeper, could tell the twins apart. She had no way to prove what she suspected, so she kept Emma's secret until she died."

Mary turned to me again. "Emma wants to talk to you," she said. "She says don't mourn for her, she is glad that her secret is out. She says she is content to be with Anna again, reunited for eternity. When she found out Anna's ghost was still here and wanted to move on, she could not bear the thought of keeping her twin from entering Heaven. She asks your forgiveness, and says she loved you like the daughter she never had."

Mary paused and remained silent for a moment.

"Anna says that she realized your mom was poisoning your dad and was trying to stop her. You were the only one receptive to her messages, and she is sorry that she scared you. She has grown very fond of you as well," Mary said.

"Emma is speaking again. She says you will be fine, just stay strong and live your life, and she wants you to know that she will always be looking out for you."

Mary moved directly behind me.

"Anna has a message for you," Mary said. "She says that in your summer bedroom, to the left of the closet, there is a small gap between the floor and the baseboard. She wants you to look there." Mary raised an eyebrow, as if confused.

"They want to approach you," Mary said.

I didn't know what to think. I was still crying, and I could not see anything.

But I felt them.

Cold fingers touched my shoulders, and I felt that cool breeze around my head. There was a sensation in my head like the pins and needles you get when your arm falls asleep. It was a strange, cold numbness that went up my neck and the back of my head.

"Emma says you will be fine, and not to be afraid," Mary said. "They are leaving now."

Tangled Trail

The chill faded away. I felt very strange, very different.

Mary put her hands on my shoulders from behind me, then kissed my cheek.

"I'm so sorry, Sweetheart," she said. "I can tell you loved her a lot, and that she loved you."

Bradley stepped out the back door. I could hear him talking on his radio.

"Are you okay?" Mary asked me.

"I don't know," I said. "I feel very strange, very light and... clear."

"You've had a long and dreadful day."

I know it had been a long day. It was closer to morning than to midnight, but I felt awake, alive.

I saw the bag of cat food on the floor where I left it.

"Lizzy," I said. I almost forgot about her again.

I took the bag and walked out the back door. Bradley was standing on the back porch, talking on his radio. Lizzy was weaving around his legs, rubbing her back against him. Maybe he was a cat person after all.

Lizzy saw me and the bag of food and came right to me. I poured some on the porch, and she sat and started eating. I scratched her back. She seemed fine.

I stepped back into the house. Bradley and Mary were talking. Bradley was awaiting a deputy, so they could go to Miss... Emma's house.

"Anna's ghost told me to check the baseboard in my room," I said to Mary. "Remember?"

"Oh, yes. You're right."

The house was still technically a crime scene, but Bradley said it was okay, and told us not to touch anything unless we had to.

Mary and I went up the creaky stairs and into my summer room. I turned on the light and looked for the gap between the floor and baseboard. It was there, just like she had said. I dropped onto my hands and knees and pushed my face against the floor, trying to get one eye at floor level.

"It's too dark to see anything," I said. I hopped up and went to the closet and retrieved a wire coat hanger. I straightened the hook. I dropped back onto my knees and fished around with the wire. With just a couple of swipes, a glint of silver caught my eye.

It was a loop of a fine silver chain. I gently pulled on it, teasing more of the chain out of the gap. I met some resistance but kept steady pressure on the chain.

"What is it?" Mary asked over my shoulder.

I continued to pull until it came free.

Half of a heart medallion lay on the floor.

I could not help but to giggle, even though there were tears in my eyes. "After all these years," I said.

Mary followed me downstairs to my bedroom. I went right to the dollhouse and pulled out the other half of the medallion. I put the two haves together on the dollhouse floor. One said *Sisters* and the other said *Forever*.

"The halves are together again," I said. "Just like the sisters... forever."

Epilogue

Of course, everything in my world changed on that day.

I still think of my friend and neighbor as Miss Anna. She had lived far longer as Anna than she had as Emma, so I think it's alright. I believe she thought of herself as Anna, so it seems fitting, even though I now know the truth.

Miss Anna was found in her garage, sitting in her running car. While she didn't drive often, she kept her car in the small garage attached to the house. Bradley and a deputy found her, as if asleep, with the oldies station playing on the radio.

Mary and Bradley stayed with me that entire night. It was after dawn when the ambulance left Tangled Trail with Miss Anna's body.

Mary was on her phone early that morning. I heard her mention my name during her conversations. She had been speaking with friends, who offered to let me stay with them until I figured something else out.

I was apprehensive about the idea—which I think any normal person would have been under the circumstances—but I had to do something.

Even though I was nervous about my immediate future, I was surprised that I was not a complete basket case. I was not only aware, but grateful that my anxiety symptoms were at a minimum.

Mary approached me with that tired, but wonderful smile of hers.

"I think we have something worked out," she said. "I'm sure you will do fine. The people I've contacted are absolutely amazing."

"Okay," I said. I was as tired as Mary looked, and even though my mind whirled at a furious pace, my body screamed for a rest.

We were still at my house. The Sheriff had allowed us to be there, even though it was still a crime scene. Never in a million years could I have foreseen the day when yellow police tape would be draped around the only two houses on Tangled Trail.

Lizzy had been hanging around the house, weaving between people's legs and begging for attention. It seemed she no longer feared the ghost, and I wondered if she somehow knew the ghost was gone.

It was time to go, and Mary and Bradley and I got into the police cruiser. We drove back to Freeport in near silence. I think everyone was so exhausted that we were all focused on some much-needed downtime.

We soon arrived at a very nice home on the edge of town. Bradley parked in the driveway, and we all got out. I carried Lizzy in my arms, the rest of my clothes still in the shopping bags in the trunk.

An older couple greeted us at the door. It took me a minute, but I recognized the woman, and grins crossed our faces at the same time.

"Hadlee!" she said. She stepped past the man she was with and reached out to me. "I haven't seen you in a long time, girl. Look how you've grown!"

She gave me a long embrace, patting my back as she did. Lizzy began squirming, fearing suffocation since she was trapped between us.

The woman put her hands on my shoulders and pushed me to arm's length, giving Lizzy a breath.

"Hi, Rosie," I said. "I didn't know I was coming to your house."

"Rosie and Stanley were the first people I thought of," Mary said. "When I told Rosie what had happened, she didn't hesitate to say yes. That was before I told her your name. She said she knew you and your family."

"This is Stanley," Rosie said.

The man stepped forward and stuck out his hand. My hands were full of cat, so he put an arm around me instead.

"Don't worry," Rosie said. "His bark is worse than his bite."

"I haven't said anything... yet," Stanley replied. "It's her you have to watch out for," he teased.

"You all look so tired," Rosie said. "And I'll bet you haven't eaten in a while. I put a breakfast casserole in the oven. It should be ready in a few minutes."

We put Lizzy in the fenced backyard, and she began to explore the new surroundings.

Breakfast was terrific. A casserole with eggs and sausage and cheese, and various cut fruit on the side.

After eating my fill, I was beginning to nod off while the adults talked.

"Sweetheart," Rosie said. "Let's show you your room so you can get some sleep."

I feared that I would not be able to sleep in strange surroundings during the day. But Rosie pulled the shades and I fell into the bed. Within moments I was asleep.

And I dreamed.

I dreamed of twin girls standing in a field, looking at what they called *their tree*. It was a lone tree in a wheat field. One of the girls wore a pale-yellow dress; the other wore the same dress in pale green. They sat in the tree's shadow, giggling, holding hands and singing nursery rhymes. In the background was the house I had lived in most of my life, but it was new and bright, gleaming in the sun.

I dreamed of my dad at a time when I was still small. He was much thinner then, and had on a carpenter's tool belt, a hammer dangling at his side. In my dream, Dad was optimistic, energetic and still had dreams of his own. He talked about how he was going to fix up that weathered house, and make it look like it did in the old days…

I did not dream of my mother, and I tried not to read anything into that. She was my mom, and I had no idea why she did what she had done. She had raised me and nurtured me, and made sure I was fed. I know she worked hard, and in turn, had taken little time to live.

But forgiveness was one thing; forgetfulness was entirely something else.

I awoke in a strange room many hours later. It was dark outside. I heard a TV playing faintly in the house.

Rosie must have heard me stirring, as she met me in the hallway.

"How are you, Sweetie?" she asked.

"A little groggy," I said, "but otherwise okay."

I found the bathroom first, then walked to the light at the end of the hall.

Stanley was in a recliner watching TV. He hit the mute button when I walked in.

Rosie had me sit down. She told me that Bradley had relayed a message that if I wanted to go to the hospital again that night, he could have a deputy escort me. Rosie told me that my dad's oxygen level had gone down during the day, and the hospital was fighting to get it higher. Rosie and Stanley both agreed to go with me if I wanted them to, and I did.

Tangled Trail

A deputy met us at the hospital and took me to my dad's room in the ICU. There were more people around than the night before, but my anxiety level seemed fine, which surprised me.

My dad looked worse than the night before. His skin was a sickly, bluish-gray. His eyes seemed sunken in. His body struggled to breathe, each breath ragged and labored.

The nurse explained that his condition had worsened, and to get any more aggressive with the treatment would be counterproductive. She said it was a waiting game now, and that they were doing all they could.

Rosie pulled a visitor chair alongside my dad's bed, where I sat for some length of time. I just held my dad's hand and talked to him, telling him how much I needed him and that I didn't want to be alone.

But I also whispered to him that I hated to see him suffer, and to do what was best for him, which caused me to break into a sobbing spell. While I didn't want to see him suffer, I was still selfishly holding the idea that somehow, things would get back to some version of normal, and we would be together again.

Dad remained unresponsive throughout my visit. I might have stayed there the entire night, but Rosie came in and put a hand on my shoulder.

"We need to go," she whispered. "The hospital has my number and will call us if anything changes. We can come back in the morning if you want to."

I kissed Dad's hand and left, feeling withdrawn and lonely.

My dad passed away the next day, on my birthday. Once the hospital had the pills that Mary O'Reilly revealed were in the house, they could target their tests and treatments more efficiently, but there was too much of the bad drug in his system. It was complicated, but something about how the drug bonded to Dad's red blood cells made it almost impossible to treat. There simply wasn't enough time to undo the effects. He never regained consciousness.

My birthday is no longer a day of celebration, only remembrance.

I felt as if I had been sucked into a giant, malevolent vortex of some kind, like one might see in a sci-fi movie. It is hard to describe, because a void, by definition, is the absence of everything. It felt as if I had been cast into a different realm, where the laws governing the universe had been changed.

Mary came to see me and offered her condolences. I could see that she felt horrible about everything I'd been through and offered to help in any way that she could.

"Can you go back to my house with me?" I asked.

She looked a little surprised at first, but then I think she knew what I really wanted.

We got permission from Sheriff Oberlin, and Bradley accompanied us to the house. We went to the kitchen, which now seemed like an alien place to me. It was different now, like a long-forgotten place being revisited.

I waited for Mary, who wandered the halls, walking slowly, listening. After what seemed a half-hour or so, she pulled out a kitchen chair.

"There is nobody here," she said. She took my hand. "Most of the time, people move on right after they die," she said. "Ghosts are the exception, not the rule."

My eyes watered up. I just knew that my dad would be there, waiting to talk to me.

"Can we wait a little longer?" I asked.

Mary nodded. "We can, but I don't think anything will change. I believe your father has moved on from his earthly ties." She squeezed my hand. "It doesn't mean he doesn't love you," she said. "Be happy for him, because this is what is supposed to happen when we die. We move on to another life, never to return."

I think I wanted to say goodbye to the old house, because I knew I would never live there again. Mary walked with me, as we went into each room. I studied each one, taking a mental picture and reliving happier moments from my life there. I was also hoping that Dad might still show up, even though I was glad thinking that he had moved on and was now happy in the afterlife.

I finally gave up and felt as though my goodbye was over. Lingering would not change the pain, which brought a Friedrich Nietzsche quote to mind. He said, *'That which doesn't kill you, makes you stronger.'*

I told Mary it was time to go.

Days went by, and each one got a tiny bit better, but progress was taken back because of the funerals. I attended two funerals for three people and relived the memories and the loss yet again. Both funerals were small, private services. Dad's only sister came, but my cousins did not. Dad's sister was no longer married, so the two of us exchanged uncomfortable niceties as a few people came and went.

Miss Anna had outlived most of her friends and had no extended family. The real Anna had never had a chance to make many friends and had been gone for a very long time.

Rosie and Stanley were incredibly gracious and looked out for me in ways that I never thought possible outside of a family.

Mary and Bradley stopped by on occasion, offering me some details about my mom. She had eventually confessed.

I talked to her once before the trial, while she was still in jail. She looked the same, outside of the orange jumpsuit. We had to talk through a telephone, where we looked at each other through a glass barrier.

I spoke first, a single word; "why?"

Mom exhaled heavily, then launched into a thousand reasons why she wanted Blake out of her life, forever.

It boiled down to her having an affair with a man she met through her work. Dad had a small life insurance policy, but she swears the money was not the motive.

111

She wanted Dad gone forever, so that she would not have to see him again. She could not imagine him being able to take care of me on his own and felt that he would have spiraled into even worse health without her to help him manage things. She believed her leaving would be something that would crush what remained of him. She didn't want to put the burden of caring for Dad on me, either, so she did what she saw as best for both of us.

It was sick and twisted, I know. But I sometimes tell myself that a desperate mind makes up its own justification. I heard the desperation in her voice. She wanted a new life, with no traces of Blake Monroe to cloud things up.

The famous last words were the same as so many others—*I didn't think I'd get caught.*

"But I want you to know that I love you, Hadlee," she said. "I love you more than anything."

I bit my lip for a moment. I wanted to hear those words, but knew they were meaningless.

"If you loved me, you would not have killed my father," I said.

I had no more to say to her but saw the first tears streak over her cheeks before I got up and left the room. She called to me... I heard her voice over the tiny speaker in the dangling handset. I did not turn back.

I was only present for a small part of Mom's trial, but Mary and Bradley kept me informed on the details. There was a chance I would have to testify, but I was told as the trial went on that it seemed less likely all the time. The lawyers did not want to expose me to that if at all possible.

Mom was convicted of murder and sentenced to fifty years in prison. I have no plans to visit her in the Dixon Correctional Center, but things could change. Never is a long time...

Miss Anna's attorney contacted me a few days after her funeral. Rosie took me to see him, where he informed me that Anna DuVall (it's who she was in the eyes of the law) had left her entire estate to me. He told me that she had not made that decision recently but had written up her most recent will more than three years prior to her death.

The money she left me was not the millions that Dad thought she had tucked away, but was enough to see me through for a long time. Rosie says the land Miss Anna owned on Tangled Trail was worth a fortune to the right developer—and being a real estate broker, she would know.

A few days later, Bradley came to visit, saying he had some business to talk about. The police had confiscated our computers, so they could search for email and any other evidence pertinent to the case.

"We ran a routine scan on your dad's computer," he said. "We found evidence of identity theft and stolen funds on his computer. I didn't want to tell you, but apparently you signed up for an online therapy class, which was paid for with stolen money."

I must have looked stupefied, so Bradley went on.

"Your dad was skimming funds through online accounts with stolen credit card numbers," he said. "Your class has been cancelled. You can be reinstated by paying the fees again." He looked away for a moment. "You would have found out," he said. "The cardholders pressed charges, and you were notified through email of the cancellation."

I had not been on a computer since I left Tangled Trail.

"I'm sorry, Hadlee," Bradley said. "But I thought it better to tell you, rather than have you find out on your own."

Everyone in my little family on Tangled Trail had a secret, it seemed.

"The Sheriff's people discovered an old cistern under your bedroom," Bradley said. "They excavated and found a body that they believe to be the real Anna DuVall." He looked up to get my reaction. "Her remains are being buried next to her sister with a single headstone with both names on it. In the eyes of the law, nobody knows which was which."

It was a bit creepy thinking that I had been sleeping above Anna DuVall's body all that time. But it did explain the sounds that came up through the pipes in my closet. I thought it was nice that Anna and Emma had been buried together, as a family.

I have a new family now. It's not a traditional family, but to be honest, I feel more a part of this family than my old one.

Rosie has computer issues, so I have been helping her out. When she found out I was a computer whiz, she praised God and put me to work. She knows other people with computer-phobia, so I keep myself pretty busy doing what I like to do.

I have a small apartment in Freeport, which keeps me close to my clients. Most of my work I can do from my apartment, on the new laptop I bought. I do a lot of website maintenance, electronic forms, and a lot of tutoring. I'm the computer-tutor in my new family.

I can't explain what happened to my anxiety issues. The symptoms have been almost non-existent since the tragedies on Tangled Trail. Maybe Mom was right—being tossed into the deep end to sink or swim may have done it. If I can live through that kind of suffering, perhaps I can live through almost anything. Maybe my coping mechanism broke back in the fourth grade, and the trauma of recent events caused a reset of some sort. Maybe I've convinced myself that nothing is as bad as it seems.

Perhaps it was Anna and Emma. When their ghosts touched me, my head felt different, as if some of the cobwebs had been swept away by their icy touch. Who knows what a touch from another dimension of existence can do?

But since that night, I have felt really good regarding to my anxiety issues. I still avoid large crowds, but I feel comfortable in small groups, and that has built my confidence a lot. I feel that life is now available to me; the chains of anxiety cast away.

Tangled Trail

And... I met this boy. I don't know him well, but he is so cute. He's a bit shy, like me, but he seems so nice. He works down the street from my apartment. He's does some kind of engineering while still working on his degree. I see him on the street and we talk. He has a large family and invited me to a cookout at his parents' place. He's also going to teach me to drive. I have things to look forward to.

It was Friedrich Nietzsche who also said, 'To live is to suffer, to survive is to find some meaning in the suffering.'

Nietzsche was a very insightful man.

What Nietzsche didn't say, is that we can make up our own meanings. We can assign the meaning that most comforts us, which is just what I do when I think about the events that unraveled on Tangled Trail.

The End

About the Author

I grew up reading and cannot imagine life without books.

Paranormal thrillers and books with a supernatural theme are what I love to read, so I try to write stories that reflect that love. I cannot imagine writing the kind of stories you can see on the news each night, although some of that is pretty scary too.

I live in rural northern Illinois and enjoy riding my bike down the country roads around my home. My wife and I have a houseboat on a lake in central Illinois, where we spend as many weekends as possible, fishing, swimming and visiting with friends.

My website is www.donnielight.com, and I have a blog there as well. I'm on Facebook regularly, so please look me up.

Thanks for reading *Tangled Trail*. I hope you enjoyed it and will consider leaving an honest review on Amazon. Please check out some of my other titles that appear on the following page.

Books by Donnie Light

Novels
Dark Justice
Delaney's Cure
Written with Shawn Weaver
Ripper's Row
Ripper's Revenge
Ripper's Wrath
Novellas
The Hotel California
True Song
Short Stories
Swamp Witch

The *Hotel California* and *Swamp Witch* are both included in the anthology *Lyrical Darkness,* along with a number of chilling stories by other authors.

Made in the USA
Columbia, SC
06 November 2023